The Folly of French Kissing

Carla McKay

GIBSON SQUARE

First published in 2012 by Gibson Square Books

www.gibsonsquare.com

ISBN: 978-1-908096-10-4

Printed by the CPI Group (UK) Ltd, Croydon, CR0 4YY

The Folly of French Kissing

Prologue

Dawn in Montpellier is not a bit like dawn in England where nothing much stirs before 8 am. It is 6 am now and already there are hundreds of start-of-the-day sounds: people sounds, traffic sounds, birdsong, wooden shutters being flung open, café canopies being cranked open along creaky rollers, metal chairs being noisily unstacked on pavements, stray dogs fighting over bits of stale bread thrown out by restaurants, the first tram scattering unwary pedestrians in the Place de la Comédie with its warning bell. Here a baby crying near an open window; there a violin warming up.

In one of the prettiest and most secretive alleys running off the square where the covered market already has thousands of gleaming aubergines and peppers and dewy peaches on display in a dozen different stalls, a man wearing a crumpled linen jacket, staggers into what looks like a hole in the wall laden with heavy boxes of books which he carries up the alleyway steps from the open boot of an old Renault van.

When he has finished this backbreaking chore and parked the Renault elsewhere, he gets a bucket and mop and, with increasing fury, attempts to scrub the nightly offerings of the local graffiti artist off his ancient wooden front door. Eventually, he gives up and goes back inside to fetch a freestanding sandwich board and places it just outside to the left of the door. In he goes again, this time to return with a large rolled up bolt of material which he carefully attaches to a rather makeshift flagpole to the right of the door. He unrolls it to reveal a large flag, the red and white and blue of which come together to form the familiar pattern of the Union Jack as the cloth catches an early morning breeze and unfurls itself properly.

This is curious enough, but if you approach the top of the alleyway, you can make out the lettering on the board which explains it all: WUTHERING HEIGHTS ENGLISH BOOKSHOP. At least, it explains it all to the many passing English tourists who, fortunately for its owner, cannot resist an English bookshop in France even though they rarely step inside one at home. The French mostly find it inexplicable and scuttle past as though they were being invited to betray their country just by glancing in.

Gerald Thornton, the bookshop's owner, meanwhile, feels like a mountaineer who has struggled to the top of some inaccessible peak and proudly planted his flag, only to be greeted with bemused if not hostile stares from the natives and sheepish grins, if lucky, from his own countrymen.

This is my corner of a foreign field that is forever England he thinks, as he contemplates another long, hot day.

1

"School for Scandal"

The London Evening News, June 5th
From our Education Correspondent:

"In the most delicate of circumstances, the deputy headmistress of a leading public school, The Chase, near Warwick, has quietly resigned after a distinguished career of 16 years. She had developed what was described as a 'schoolgirl crush' on the headmistress, Mrs Veronica Templeton.

It appears that Miss Judith Hay, 38, had developed an obsessive affection for Mrs Templeton, 52, who was only appointed to the post at the beginning of the Spring term. The friendship took the form of poems of endearment and it is believed that when this became known, some of the parents took the matter into their own hands and informed the school governors who accepted Miss Hay's resignation with immediate effect.

Mrs Templeton confirmed: 'It is true that Judith Hay has written a lot of poetry and I have seen some of it. An awkward situation has arisen but I would like to remind everyone of the devoted service Miss Hay has given to the school over a long period. She will be sadly missed.'

The Chase, in common with many of our foremost boarding schools, has seen a slump in numbers in recent years, but Mrs Templeton is expected to reverse the trend. Sir Charles Forres, the chairman of the governors of the school, commented: 'The appointment of Veronica Templeton in January this year has already paid tremendous dividends and we can look forward with renewed confidence. We have acted in the best interests of the school in putting this unfortunate incident behind us, and now we should like to get on with providing the first-class education for which we are known.'

Old girls of The Chase include the High Court Judge, Miss Mary Owen-Wright and the actress June Lafitte.

Miss Hay, who is believed to be staying with friends in London, was unavailable for comment."

2

Tim Lavery was probably in the wrong job. He had landed the post of features writer on the *Tribune* about three months previously and, to be honest, he was a bit out of his depth. He had been able to cope pretty well on his London local paper, but a national paper, especially the *Tribune*, a tough middle-market tabloid (motto: 'We Deliver'), was he discovered rather more demanding. The name of the game as Gisella, the loathsome features editor, kept reminding him, was to be 'proactive', a buzz word Tim thought, that she had quite possibly picked up from the marketing department. 'Ideas, Tim, ideas!', she would shriek at him in morning conference. Tim did his best, but it clearly wasn't good enough judging from Gisella's daily wrath and the pitying glances of some of Gisella's hag-like cronies on the aptly named Self pages (Me, my breasts, my fitness regime, my boyfriend, my little money worries and even more about Me tomorrow). Why, he thought, on especially bad days, had he not heeded his mother's advice and become a fireman? At least the story came to you.

As if he didn't have enough on his plate. His personal life was in bad shape too. Tim's latest Fulham floozie, a rather louche little number called Scarlet, who had more money than sense, had done a bunk that weekend saying she didn't want to be his cleaner, mummy and secretary, as well as his mistress. OK, perhaps she had more sense than money. With his floppy hair and poetry books and guitar strumming, Tim found plenty of girls – no problem. Keeping them was more difficult.

When he thought no-one was looking he flicked through the book his stepmother had slipped into his stocking last Christmas: *Stop getting Dumped*. Christ, was it that obvious? 'I've got your best interests at heart, darling,' she trilled. Your father had the same problem till he met me!' It was full of brilliant advice that Tim had no intention of following like 'Always send flowers after a successful date.' What crap, Tim thought. If it had been successful you would be under her duvet and she would be making you a cup of tea before going off to work. Flowers would be a complete waste of everyone's time and money.

Now he was sitting at his desk chewing a biro top which turned his teeth a fetching shade of royal blue and, once again, wondering what he could offer up in conference to titillate the coven. It was June and outside he could see that it was deliciously hot judging from the steady stream of the fortunate unemployed clad in the stylish British summer uniform of vest and shorts turning into Kensington Gardens to give themselves a grilling. Bugger this for a lark, he thought. I've got to find something that'll get me on the road and out of this damn office. What he'd really like to do now, apart from joining the great unwashed in the park, was to get on the internet and explore some of the chat rooms but there was no damn privacy here in the open plan office.

It was like Waterloo station with a constant stream of people walking past, carrying coffee in paper cups, chatting on the edge of each others' desks and shouting into the telephone. Every so often Gisella, separate from the mere hacks in her transparent box cubicle at the end of the room, would look up and give him the evil eye. When this happened, Tim would pick up his phone and speak urgently to himself. Now he saw her put down one of her telephones and start her perambulations around the office prior to conference. Swiftly he started to look through last night's evening papers hoping to pick up a news story that could possibly trigger a feature.

'School for Scandal'. He read the headline in the *Evening News* and then chuckled as he read the story. The Chase was the school that Scarlet had been chucked out of if he remembered rightly. He then turned to that morning's scandal sheet, *The Star*. What had been a rather muted story with just a hint of prurient innuendo in the *Evening News* had been blown up in torrid tabloid fashion in *The Star*. 'Sapphic Sex Shock at Top Totties' Boarding School' screamed its headline accompanied by a completely irrelevant glamour photograph of June Lafitte, a former pupil who was now a topless model.

Gisella hovered near his desk. 'Anything in the papers?', she asked idly. Tim showed her the school story. 'Perhaps I should go up there and do a background feature on lesbian antics at our top girls' schools,' he suggested. 'Good idea,' drawled Gisella. 'Get as much steamy sex detail as you can and then wax indignant about declining morals, corruption of young, yada yada, and demand some action – you know the kind of thing – where is the Church of England when we need it? – and so on. There's not much else happening, god knows. Go up there this afternoon and speak to as many people as possible.' She looked again at the *Evening News* report. 'The Hay woman has scarpered to London according to this – I'll get the news desk on to her, if they aren't already. They can find out who her friends are and doorstep them. You get the girl-on-girl action in the dorms and see if you can talk to the Templeton woman. If she won't squeal, you can try to talk to other members of the staff. See how much they all knew and get an idea of how much of this kind of stuff goes on there. Take a photographer with you and at least get some shots of the pretty ones.'

Hurray! He was out of the office. He could drive up to Warwickshire in a leisurely way, perhaps stopping at a country pub en route and then spend a pleasant afternoon being confided in by sex-starved schoolgirls – wait till they got their hands on a real man, he thought. That's obviously what those little minxes need….

Some hours later, fortified by a ploughman's and a couple

of pints, Tim arrived at The Chase, a Victorian gothic monstrosity closely resembling Dotheboys Hall. Only here, it was Dothegirls. Ha! He felt a headline coming on. Cheerfully, he rang the brass bell, realising as he did so that he hadn't really given a thought as to how he would tackle the monstrous regiment of women within on their sexual proclivities. God, this could be tricky. Minutes passed and finally a fussy-looking woman appeared. 'Can I help you?' She peered at him over her pince-nez spectacles. Tim explained who he was and asked in what he imagined was a voice of firm authority to see Mrs Templeton.

The tweedy woman made a moué of distaste at the words *Tribune* and told him sharply to wait where he was. When she came back she told him Mrs Templeton would not see him, had no comment to make, and would like him to leave the premises immediately. Part of Tim was obscurely relieved. What was he going to say to the woman, anyhow, even if she had appeared – 'Good Afternoon, Madam, are you perchance a Citizen of Lesbos? And what about your good handmaidens here? Any chance of some action shots?'

Fortunately, he had left that gorilla of a photographer, Ron, in the car. Better to keep him out of sight for a bit. He really would put the wind up these tweedy termagants. He wandered round to the side of the building hoping to catch someone outside the school. In the distance he could see girls darting around a games pitch waving what looked like fishing nets over their heads. Blimey, what game was that?

Or was it an ancient fertility rite? Dimly, he recalled the existence of lacrosse. This was like stepping into a time warp! He wondered if he could weave lacrosse sticks into his piece – it would give it a raffish, Angela-Brazil-meets-Emmanuelle air: 'Cradle, girls, cradle!'

A side door opened and a woman came out and made for the car park. Tim bounded up to her. 'Excuse me, are you a member of staff?' The woman turned, trying to control a look of annoyance. 'I am, can I help, she asked briskly. 'Um, I wonder if you could spare me a few minutes to talk generally about The Chase,' started Tim. 'We, at the *Tribune*, would very much like to set the record straight. Of course, I'm referring to the sensationalist stories that have appeared in the gutter press this morning.' The woman's polite smile froze. 'I mean, I expect you've got a few things to say about that, haven't you?' he added hopefully. 'If you like, we could talk somewhere else off the record.'

The woman now visibly shuddered. 'I'm not in the habit of talking to the press,' she now said sternly. 'And you won't find anyone else here is either. Does the headmistress know you're here?' 'Yes, she does,' said Tim truthfully. 'I only want to establish the facts about why Miss Hay had to leave and whether this kind of thing goes on much here?'

'I have no idea 'what kind of thing' you're referring to,' said the woman coldly. 'And now I think you'd better go.' She turned on her heel.

Tim saw that it was hopeless. 'The kind of thing I mean,' he yelled after her, 'is lesbian lust, romps in the dorm, seduction in the staffroom – just the usual', his voice trailed off as the door slammed.

Damn, he thought. Why didn't I think this thing through? I should have pretended that I'm a prospective parent. Then I'd have been in the Head's study in a flash with a prospectus in one hand and a direct debit form in the other. Now I've gone and alerted the whole school to the fact that I'm a hack and the next thing will be that I'll be escorted out of here by a posse of Latin teachers with moustaches.

He started off back towards his car where he could see Ron the photographer with his feet up on the dashboard lighting up another fag. Better get the gorilla out to take some snaps of Dracula's Castle at least, he thought, before it's too late. Ron eased himself out of the passenger seat, paunch first. 'Aven't seen any posh tottie, yet', he complained. 'Where are all these porn queens then? I wos looking forward to taking some "snatch" shots.' 'He laughed wheezily. 'Very funny,' replied Tim. 'They're all locked up in there waiting for a god like you to rescue them. Let's take some pics of the school of shame and then go into the town and see what we can learn there.'

This turned out to be more fruitful. In town Tim spotted small groups of Chase girls – sixth formers probably in their mushy pea blazers– mooching around the shops. He approached one such group who giggled nervously when he explained who he was and that he was doing a newspaper article on The Chase and wanted some background information. One of them, who volunteered that her name was Carinthia, seemed bolder than the rest – certainly if her skirt length was anything to go by. 'Do any of you want to come and have a cup of tea with me and fill me in on school life', he asked engagingly. 'Sure', said Carinthia. 'I don't have to be back till five. I'll see you two later,' she told the others.

Once they were out of earshot, she said to Tim, 'Can we make it a drink at the bar round the corner – and do you have a cigarette on you?' This was promising, thought Tim as he ordered Carinthia a whisky and coke and himself another beer. 'What do you want to know?' asked Carinthia flirtatiously lighting up a cigarette and blowing newly perfected smoke rings in his face. 'The school's rubbish. I can't wait to leave.'

For a while she chatted happily enough about the tedium of school life and the ridiculous way they were made to work so hard and had no social life at all. Tim nodded sympathetically occasionally making notes. Gradually he brought the conversation round to boyfriends. 'Don't you all miss your boyfriends whilst you're locked up at school?' he asked. 'God yes,' affirmed Carinthia. 'By week seven of term we're all lusting after the handyman who's got a hunch back, or someone random like that.' This was his cue. 'Do, um, do some of you…' Tim felt unexpectedly shy in the presence of this attractive and precocious schoolgirl who kept provocatively tossing back her long hair which she had released from its ponytail. 'That's to say, do some of you ever… er… turn to each other in this situation?' he blurted out finally.

Carinthia made a face. 'Yu-uk. What are you suggesting? That we all leap into bed with each other?' 'Er, yes,' said Tim. 'I mean that would be perfectly understandable given the lack of men. I expect a lot of that goes on in a girls' boarding school doesn't it?' He looked hopefully at Carinthia. 'No', she said. 'Well, if it does, I've never seen any of it, and wouldn't want to. It goes on in boys' boarding schools of course but my friends and I are crazy about our boyfriends. We talk about them all the time and we'd never think of doing anything with each other. That would be so gross.'

'What about the teachers then?' asked Tim. 'They're mostly old spinsters, aren't they? What do they get up to? Look at Miss Hay – she's had to leave because of it.'

Carinthia looked bored. 'I don't honestly know what they do,' she said. 'Look at them, though, they're all old and as ugly as sin. I should think sex is the last thing on their minds – they wouldn't even know what it was.'

'But Miss Hay?' Tim persisted. Carinthia looked doubtful. 'I really don't know why she's gone,' she said. 'There's been rumours that she got too close to the Head and wrote romantic stuff to her but I find that hard to believe. Of all of them, she was probably the most normal. A bit quiet and shy but really nice when you got to know her. And she was a good English teacher. I'm quite sorry she's gone actually.'

This was most definitely not what Tim wanted to hear. He decided to come clean with Carinthia – she was clearly the kind of girl who could take it. 'Look Carinthia,' he said. 'To be honest, my paper wants me to write an article, based on this story of Miss Hay which is in the papers today, about lesbianism in girls boarding schools – the more the merrier as far as they're concerned. Couldn't you just embellish some stories for me with authentic detail so that it sounds right about what you all get up to in the showers and so on? I'll even pay you for it.'

An hour later, Tim had enough material for his feature and Carinthia had a fresh packet of cigarettes and a tenner. It was well worth it. She even posed for a photograph for Ron on condition that it was made clear that she was not one of the Sapphic sisters that the newspaper had somehow got to hear about.

Her vanity was, of course, to be her downfall when Tim's piece appeared two days later ('Not so Chaste at The Chase'). In the mayhem that followed with the parents and governors up in arms and a Spanish Inquisition in the school as to who was the 'mole', Carinthia confessed. She had been the obvious suspect after all with her picture in the paper (she was pleased about that).

The school made a formal complaint to the *Tribune* and the Press Complaints Commission. Their case was clear-cut. A reporter had bribed a schoolgirl to give him an entirely false account of events at The Chase. The newspaper was forced to apologise on its front page the following day. Tim was told to clear his desk and was actually escorted from the building by Cyril the security guard. 'Seems a shame,' Cyril said companionably, as they went down in the lift together. 'You wos only doing your job. That's what this game is about, innit? Making up stories.'

Tim agreed it was a pity. 'Best piece I ever did, Cyril', he said. Really, he had to laugh. Gisella had actually shaken her fist at him through her glass partition as he packed up to go. He supposed her head was on the line now too. She had been crazy about the piece. 'None of the others seem to have got a sniff of this,' she said. 'Well done, Tim, I always thought you could do it.'

At about the time Tim was ruefully handing in his office car keys to the reception desk downstairs, Carinthia was insouciantly clambering into her parents' BMW with her trunk on the roof rack for what should have been a shamefaced journey home for the final time.

In fact, neither she nor Tim, it has to be said, much minded leaving their respective institutions in disgrace. Both felt that they probably faced a brighter future because of it.

3

As usual, Judith crash-landed into consciousness, her heart hammering, her sheet twisted. She lay there deep-breathing for a few more minutes, willing her clenched muscles to relax, trying to drive off the butterflies that seemed to nest perpetually in her stomach.

I'm here now; I'm safe, she told herself. I'm not there. I'm here, in France and I've got to stop thinking about it. Physical pain would have been easier; it would have been over by now and forgotten about. Shame, it seemed, lingered longer. It might never leave her.

In the crippling aftermath of her ignominious 'retirement' from The Chase, she had lain low in London for a while, paralysed by misery and indecision. But even London wasn't far enough away. Like so many others whose lives have taken a wrong turn, she had opted to start again in a new country, thinking it would make all the difference.

Now, here in rural France – only a few days after the news reports but seemingly a lifetime away – the sun streamed in through a chink in the shutters; it was that which had awoken her. It's strange, she mused, how I longed for this sun. I thought it would heal me and bring me some peace, but it's not so. Back in England, it's all anybody thinks about – it's absence anyway. In all the 'olive n' vine' books and holiday programmes featuring farmhouses, swimming pools and lavender, the sun is the facilitator of a happy and blessed existence. But, sadly, you finally learn that you can move all you like, but you take your baggage with you. All those lifestyle programmes at home with titles like 'No Turning Back' now seemed apocalyptic and threatening.

It wasn't that she wanted to be back in England particularly; she appreciated all kinds of things about France. It was just that her move here hadn't really solved anything or, as yet, brought her any lasting contentment. She wondered how many others in the growing expatriate community out here felt the same. God knows, there were enough of them who were finding life pretty challenging. It was probably why they all stuck together like glue.

Thinking of this, she suddenly realised that it was Saturday, which meant two things: the first, market day in Vevey, an enjoyable outing important for socialising and linguistic skills as well as procuring anything from groceries to an ironing board cover. The second was far less inviting. In the evening, and there was no escaping this, there was the dreaded barbeque.

The Saturday barbeque had become an institution among the expatriate community, always held at one of their houses in the area by prearrangement. When Judith had first come to La Prairie, a medieval village close to the sizeable market town of Vevey, she had marvelled at how many other British people had migrated to the region. There must have been a shifting population of about three hundred of them in her village and a few of the neighbouring ones. Naturally they gravitated towards each other and formed a loose alliance. Many of them didn't speak French, nor even made an effort to do so, but even those who did found it difficult to integrate locally and would have been lost without their fellow countrymen.

Any newcomer was fallen upon with a degree of delight and there was little chance of avoiding them. One could have gone out every night to drinks, to supper or to the local bridge club even, and many did. Many of these invitations in the early days, Judith wisely declined, but it was impossible not to show up sometimes at the Saturday event.

A solitary person, by inclination and temperament, Judith had at first been horrified by such enforced intimacy with people, most of whom she would certainly have avoided knowing at home. A year on, the horror had largely given way to boredom, but even she had to acknowledge that the ex-pats represented a useful support system and she knew she should be more grateful for their overtures of friendship.

And, she had to admit, some of them were perfectly OK. She hadn't really made a proper friend yet nor felt there were any kindred spirits to whom she could really relate, but she wasn't overly concerned. There were those, however, whom she positively didn't want to know. With a shudder she thought now of Lance Campion, the unofficial and self-elected 'leader' in his late forties of the Britpack as he called it.

After apparently making bundles of money in advertising, Lance had taken early retirement to the South of France and had written one of the early books on the good life in the sun which had bought him modest celebrity. The fact that he was so pleased with himself took the edge off his leonine good looks, and Judith thought him calculating and opportunist rather than clever. He was one of those people who invaded your space, both physically and mentally. He made her very nervous, and like a dog which shies away from certain people, she knew that she couldn't conceal her dislike. And he sensed it.

The last time she had seen him at a dinner party, he had fixed her with his oddly pale eyes towards the end of the evening: 'What are you running away from Judith?' he asked in a conspiratorial voice, low enough not to be overheard. She felt herself go cold and after a beat too long had forced herself to answer in what she hoped was a light-hearted manner. 'Do I look as though I'm running away, Lance? 'You do', he replied and turned away. He didn't need to say, 'And I intend to find out.' Lance didn't like secrets – other people's at any rate. Please god let him not be there tonight.

Vevey was heaving. The entire length of the town's longest

street culminating in the Place de la République gave way to the market. It was difficult to move. Judith joined the hordes of perambulating people in much the same way as a car from a sliproad finally forces its way into a gap on the *Autoroute*. Hundreds of determined French housewives, most carrying the obligatory baguette under their arm which usefully doubled as a crowd control weapon, shouted up at stallholders for cheese, for fruit, for Toulouse sausages, for flowers, or just shouted at each other. Shouting, Judith noted, was the norm here. God knows what they did when they were angry. At first, she, like all the more reticent British, mumbled her requests at the vendors but it was useless. She could speak French more or less fluently, but in the *Midi*, the South of France, it was ineffectual as a tool of communication unless it was delivered at mega decibels. Other English residents seemed to have caught on to this too. Quite often – disturbingly often in fact – Judith could hear her fellow countrymen bellowing for oysters or ordering a coffee in voices that used to be reserved for running the empire.

There was a brisk trade in overalls, the kind French housewives don in order to scrub their front steps. An awful lot of them were actually wearing the things, along with their slippers. Funny how the French had a reputation for chic clothes, Judith mused. It certainly wasn't in evidence round here. But then, until recently nobody had really heard of the Languedoc and both the region and its inhabitants seemed largely untouched by contemporary life.

This huge sleepy area to the west of Provence – every inch of it covered with vines and three times the size of the celebrated Bordeaux region – was the source, she had read, of one in 11 bottles of the world's wine. It had lain undiscovered, basking in the sun, by the French and foreigners alike, until about 30 years previously when a few resourceful vineyard owners recognising the terrain's potential for producing world class wines, brought in young, enthusiastic winemakers, largely from the New World, to replant the vines and apply new production methods. The startlingly good results had taken everybody by surprise and seen a huge influx in recent years of refugees from northern France as well as Britain, Germany and Holland attracted to the region by its space, climate and renewed commercial opportunities. Many of them now seemed to be in Vevey market, she reflected ruefully.

It was past midday when, feeling particularly sticky, she wandered off the main drag and into the historic heart of the town thinking she would find a café in the shade away from all the bustle. Her mind in neutral, she found herself dawdling in a part of town she didn't know very well. Here the alleyways were darker and narrower and there were no shops, just houses either side and washing hanging out on lines above her. Off the alleyway in which she found herself were several impasses – small cul-de-sacs – and glancing to her left down one of these as she strolled, she froze for a split second as she took in two people she knew rather well in a passionate clinch. Recognition gave way to shock at the scene she had witnessed. Rapidly and as noiselessly as she could, she half sprinted down the alley and rounded the corner into a small square at the top. There she paused to catch her breath before hurrying back to the main thoroughfare another way, unable to compute in her mind the meaning of what she'd seen until she was safe amongst the crowd.

Once there, she took a table in the nearest café and ordered an espresso which she drained with shaky hands. Could she have been mistaken? No, she didn't think she could. Could she have misinterpreted what she saw? No, again. In which case, she thought, her brain firing like a scattergun, what shall I do about it? Shall I tell someone, or shall I keep quiet? Then something even worse occurred to her: supposing she herself had been seen? Now suddenly she knew with absolute icy certainty that this was the case. Small wonder she was so upset. Upset, though, wasn't the word. She had to admit it, it was something more akin to fear that she felt.

Later, after a feverish siesta – a laudable French tradition – from which she awoke unrefreshed and unresolved, she lay in bed reading her new Margaret Atwood novel. Reading was usually balm to jangling nerves but this latest Atwood was a highly disturbing glimpse into the future. Generally Judith, for whom reading was as necessary as breathing, welcomed any chance to break out of the confines of her own limited experience into another world, whether it was eighteenth century rural England or twentieth century

Chicago mean streets. This time, though, the empathetic alarm she felt for Atwood's protagonist, Jimmy, stranded alone in an alien future, dovetailed with her own sense of panic and served only to enhance it.

I too am alone, she thought a touch melodramatically. Not, it's true, in an alien future, but in an alien land to some extent. For all its proximity to Britain, France, especially here in the south, was very foreign indeed. And even in England, she had always somehow felt an onlooker, never part of the crowd. Glumly, she reviewed her life so far: the only child of rather elderly, timid parents who lived extremely quietly in a run-down terrace in Wimbledon, her childhood had been dull and conformist. Her schooling, at a local selective high school was traditional and unexceptional. An intelligent, sensitive girl, she had cruised through academically, always doing what was expected of her and never drawing attention to herself. Friends weren't encouraged at home; nor would Judith have wished to bring anyone back to the stifling atmosphere of her house where nothing, especially not her parents, had changed in forty years.

Her escape, her salvation, was her imagination to which she was able to give full rein in books, in the magical universe of the unreal – or at least other people's 'real'. How can other people not read, she had always thought? How can they learn anything from their own necessarily limited experience? How can they not want to escape from the here and now of their own lives, the dreary predictability and banality of it all?

Amongst her new acquaintances here reading as a pastime – as a lifeline – was largely dismissed: responses ranged from puzzled – 'how do you find the time?' to witty chat up lines like 'why read about it when you can do it?' or 'what's a lovely lady like you doing burrowing in books when you could be out enjoying yourself?' to that of her engaging odd job man Pete: 'Books? They do my head in.'

A degree in English Literature at University College, London, had followed school as both she and her teachers had known it would. There was no spare money for university accommodation or sharing a flat with other students (what forbidden careless rapture that would have been!) so Judith continued to live at home and life changed not a whit. What a good thing, she thought now, she had also become interested in French literature at university and had mastered the language too. That stood her in good stead here.

Also at university, Judith had become seriously interested in poetry. She responded to its haunting rhythms, its ability to convey a universal truth in a phrase, its melancholic or joyful beauty. In her spare time she tried to write it herself and found that she had a gift for it. A suitable pastime for a solitary spinster she told herself wryly. But it was more than a hobby. After successfully contributing to specialist magazines, Judith was now a published poet with three collections out and a respectful following. Being Judith though, it was only her editor and a couple of friends who realised that she wrote under the pseudonym Howard Hill, known to be a mysterious recluse who would never agree to public readings of his work.

After graduating, she had applied for and got the first post she had seen advertised: a teacher at a big girls' independent boarding school in the Midlands. The job was attractive because it came with a small flat at the school and by this time Judith thought she would surely implode if she had to spend any more time in Wimbledon.

Shortly after she left home, both her parents died, one soon after the other, tidily and without fuss. Judith was sad, but not unduly distressed. If anything, she felt liberated. The house, she sold for a useful though not considerable sum which she lodged in a building society and almost forgot about. Her requirements were pretty modest, but it did mean she could afford leisurely holidays mostly in France when The Chase broke up for the summer. The Chase, she thought now, as the butterflies returned to swarm in her stomach. No, she would not go there in her head. There was enough going on here.

4

'Early evening in the south of France in late May when the real heat has gone out of the day but the sun lingers to bathe in a golden glow the rows upon rows of young vines in leaf bordered by banks of wild iris or oleander bushes is my favourite time…', – from *Love at First Sight: A Year in the Languedoc* by Lance Campion.

It *is* very beautiful thought Judith as she drove along the narrow lanes between vineyards stretching as far as the eye could see, but a recent reading of Lance's mushy book had somehow taken the edge off its charm for her. What he failed to say was that early evening was also the time when he and his cronies start pouring themselves gin and tonics or tumbler-sized glasses of the seductively cheap local wine and congratulate each other on being clever enough to wind up down here for their retirement instead of putrefying in Purley.

Oh hell, she really must stop being so churlish. Just lately, everything seemed to have got on top of her. She supposed it was partly because she didn't really have enough to occupy herself, in spite of taking on some freelance teaching, and partly because she had yet to meet any kindred spirits. Just one would do. Even so, she was irritated by her own negativity. Grow up, she told herself sternly. I'm really very lucky to have any friends at all, and it doesn't bear thinking about what I'd be doing now if I were back in England.

After all, what do I miss? The weather? I think not. The people? Well, only a handful. Jane, in particular, a friend from university who had surprised everybody by marrying a rather glitzy banker shortly afterwards and living between London and New York. Jane had been brilliant last year when everything had gone so wrong and Judith had taken refuge with her whilst planning her escape to France. She hadn't asked Judith for details about what happened. She just accepted that Judith didn't want to discuss it and just needed somewhere to hide away until she decided upon a plan of action. Yes, she missed Jane enormously, and it was true that there was a close friend-shaped hole in her life right now, one unlikely to be filled tonight. Oh god, there I go again.

She could hear them all before she could see them. There must have been around twenty people in the pretty courtyard garden belonging to a retired wine merchant and his wife from Shropshire, Alan and Jenny Knight. 'Ah, Judith, welcome', Alan advanced towards her at the gate as she hung back surveying the scene, the smoky smell of grilled meat – not again! – drowning out the more delicate scents of the freshly sprinkled garden. 'We're trying out a new red from the wine *cave* co-operative down the road. Pierre tipped me the wink that this one's going to be the big seller this summer. Want to try some?'

'Bloody good plonk, if you ask me,' added Tony Parsons unhelpfully behind him. Tony was the man everyone used to fix their digital televisions. There was some scam whereby you could access Sky without paying for it. And, of course, watching French TV really wasn't an option. 'But it all is down here, isn't that right, Judy? And all at a knock-down price too! Managed to tear yourself away from your books then?'

Already Judith wanted to scream. How had she got herself this ghastly donnish reputation? She must have made the mistake of talking too enthusiastically about what she was reading, or what she was looking forward to reading, at some supper party in the early days. When all the time she should have been gossiping about reality TV shows and how you could tune into Big Brother on Sky if you bought a digibox over from England and got Tony to tweak it all so that it worked in France.

A little wildly she looked round for help. Somebody spare me from Tony please. Oh Christ, there was Lance advancing. 'Judith, my dear, what a pleasure'. The manner, as ever, was treacly; the eyes cold. 'And what have you been up to today?' The effrontery, thought Judith. She felt her mouth go dry. How can he ask me that when he knows damn well where I was today, and what I saw. Or does he?

If he's bluffing, I'll have to do the same.

'Nothing special,' she said, willing herself to look up at him, 'just the market in the morning.'

'Oh yes? See anyone you know? Anything interesting happening?' Lance raked his hand through his still admirably thick mane of hair.

'No, not really.' A pause. 'Although, come to think of it, I thought I saw you?' A deadly calm suddenly descended on Judith. I've got to see this thing through, she thought. I won't be bullied by this man whom I think is despicable. I've got to let him know that I saw him today and deal with the consequences or I'll never forgive myself.

'Really, where? I only slipped out for a baguette early on.'

'In the historic quarter towards noon. I got a bit lost and thought I glimpsed you down one of the side streets.'

'I don't think so.'

'Yes, I'm almost sure of it. You were with Sophie weren't you?' Lance's eyes registered this information but he said nothing. For a second Judith thought he was just going to walk away. Deliberately, he turned his back for a moment and put his wineglass down. Then he did something unexpected. He threw back his head and roared with laughter. An onlooker might have supposed the laughter to be genuine. Lance was theatrical at the best of times and he loved to strike a pose.

'Oh Judith, Judith", he gasped, as though she had said something irresistibly comic. 'You are so fanciful. That's what comes of reading too many books. You see things that aren't really there. What would I have been doing in the historic quarter with Sophie of all people? You must be mistaken.'

Judith managed a careless shrug. 'Perhaps so, but I could've sworn it was you.'

The laughter stopped. Lance brought his face very close down to hers. His pale eyes bulged slightly and his breath was laced with wine. 'Judith. Listen to me. You were mistaken.' The last three words were heavily stressed. All trace of humour had vanished and his voice had dropped to little more than a hiss.

But before Judith could escape, Lance gripped her wrist and called cheerily to his wife who could now be seen approaching, waving a napkin.

'The food's ready', she called. 'Jenny wants us to start eating.'

'Jean,' shouted Lance. 'Just a minute. Judith here swears she saw me in Vevey this morning. But apart from getting the bread, I was gardening at home wasn't I?'

'Well, you certainly did some gardening dear,' affirmed Jean. 'Although he can't really tell the plants from the weeds,' she told Judith. 'Especially out here. I had to replant a beautiful shrub he'd pulled up thinking it was just a large weed. But it's so dispiriting – gardening I mean – in this heat. Everything dies unless you water it every ten minutes. I'm beginning to think I should just create a cactus corner and have done with it. Do you have any nice things on your roof terrace, Judith?'

'No… no, I don't really. Just a couple of tubs of geraniums, but then that's all I ever had at home too,' mumbled Judith. She felt sick. 'Excuse me, Jean, I must find a drink, I'm parched.'

Slumped on a swingseat in the darkest corner of the Knights' courtyard, Rose found it hard to keep her eyes open – not because she was tired, but because she was so-oo-ooo bored. This was her half term, dammit, yet her parents had insisted that she come to bloody France with them away from all her friends and with nothing to do but trail around so-called picturesque villages which looked to her as though they were falling down with age and quaff gallons of wine (them, not her) in godforsaken bars.

But the evenings were the worst. Not for her chilling in front of satellite TV. No, of course not. They, of all their friends, had opted only for French telly so as to improve their language skills and French telly, even Rose could tell, was ludicrous. You could see that the sitcoms were totally unfunny and the wall-to-wall game shows were even worse than the English ones.

Tonight was the absolute pits. This was the third evening out this week, each one featuring more or less the same cast of people well over fifty like her parents. The formula was the same too: first fifteen minutes people fussing over whether she'd like wine – 'I'm not sure you're old enough young lady!' – or a soft drink (no Bacardi breezers here) followed up by terrible old farts with stained teeth and winey breath asking her what GCSEs (or O levels as they insisted on calling them) she was doing. Next bit was spent not listening to her reply (if she was lucky) and banging on about standards slipping, or, worse, latching on randomly to one of her subjects, say Geography, and quizzing her about the syllabus.

A couple of nights back she'd had that pompous prat Lance something or other who was supposed to have written some stupid book grilling her about Eng. Lit. Oh my god, that was the worst. First she couldn't remember which set books she was doing; then when she finally recalled that her Shakespeare was Romeo and Juliet, he had launched into a terrible rendering of the balcony scene and asked her opinion of young forbidden love… p-lease!

Now she could see him chatting up Sophie Stanhope who actually appeared to be giving him the time of day. Sophie was another unwelcome addition to the holiday. She was also fifteen and over here with her parents for half term from her boarding school in England, so naturally everyone thought it would be fun for them to be friends.

God. First of all, Sophie was desperately pretty and didn't she just know it. The streaked blonde hair, tossed around the whole time like she was some bleeding foal; the long thin legs ending up in a lacy thong (visible above her denim micro-kilt from New Look – Rose would kill for one of those); the sloaney voice together with the assured opinions that came with it and the just discernible scorn reserved for anyone who wasn't Sophie Stanhope, wasn't predicted a raft of A grades at GCSEs, and didn't attend St Mary's, the girls of which were the preferred choice of anyone at Eton or Harrow.

Hate, hate, hate, thought Rose. As if life isn't foul enough, I've now got all these idiots making comparisons between me and her and feeling sorry for me no doubt. She glanced over to where Sophie was and noted with interest, and then growing distaste, how Lance kept patting her bottom when he thought no-one was looking. Gross!

It was then that she recalled a conversation they had had the first day they had been unwillingly introduced. Rose had been asked over to Sophie's place, a fabulous farmhouse with green shutters and a large swimming pool, natch. Sitting in the textbook French farmhouse kitchen with all the trappings dear to the hearts of people like the Stanhopes who probably knew Peter Mayle's books off by heart, Sophie had offered Rose a coffee.

'Real, or instant?'

'Oh, um, what are you having?'

'I only drink real. Can't stand the stuff that passes for coffee in jars.'

Sophisticated bitch, thought Rose. 'Oh, well, I'll have the same then,' she said. 'I'm more used to instant though because it's all we have in the kitchen at school where we make toast and stuff at night.'

Sophie didn't turn round. 'Which school do you go to?'

'Mayfield Lodge'.

'Never heard of it. I'm at St Mary's. We all bring back any food and drink we like. You should see the hampers of things arriving at the beginning of term. We all pig out on *foie gras* we've brought back from holiday till that runs out. After that it's coffee and fags till somebody's boyfriend manages to get us in fresh supplies.'

'Do you have a boyfriend?' asked Rose tentatively, knowing as she did so that this was fool's territory for her.

'Oh, I've got dozens of little Etonians running after me,' said Sophie, 'but I can't be doing with it. You?'

'Oh, well, yes, sort of. At least I really like him and I think he likes me. He told my friend Angie that he thought I was really fit.'

At this Sophie ran an expert eye over Rose's stocky little body, created, Rose thought mournfully for hockey prowess rather than romance. 'Really?' She said disbelievingly. 'What's his name?'

'Paul', said Rose. 'Paul Wilson. He goes to Malvern.'

'Don't know him, I'm afraid,' said Sophie (as if she would!). 'I prefer older men myself. Snotty little schoolboys aren't really my scene.'

Well, thought Rose now, she's certainly got her older man. She watched as Tony, the TV aerial fixer extraordinaire, joined Sophie and Lance in their corner of the garden and

Sophie turned away. She evidently wasn't going to waste her thousand kilowatt smile on someone she would think of as a pleb. Lance, though, was someone Sophie would have thought worth cultivating. He was rich for one thing, having made a small fortune in the advertising business before he retired to France. For another, he was handsome in a wealthy-middle-aged-man-way she supposed. He had very light blue eyes, a lot of fair hair, a deep tan, and nice hands which he used expressively like a Frenchman. And thirdly, he was celebrated as a local author.

Since Sophie's father Rex Stanhope was some big shot publisher in London when he wasn't tending his vines down here, Sophie probably thought that was some big deal.

Idly, Sophie looked her way. Rose got up and walked towards her. 'Do you fancy going inside and listening to some music or watching telly?' she asked. 'Mrs Knight said we could'.

'Not right now, thanks, there's someone I've got to phone', replied Sophie fishing out her mobile and grimacing at Lance. 'I'll see you later though.'

Deflated, Rose went and helped herself to another sausage. 'I want to go back to England,' she thought desperately. 'Even school's better than this.'

5

Jenny Knight, having finished setting out the salads whilst her husband Alan sweated over the meat, was busy trying to introduce the newcomers Bill and Bryony Bailey to everyone else. It was proving a bit of an uphill struggle. These two had been gossiped about for months before their arrival because they had managed to purchase the grandest house in the immediate region, a sort of cross between a manor house and a chateau with 18 bedrooms, river frontage and many hectares of old vines.

Several agents had been involved in the lengthy and difficult transactions, one of whom was the local English estate agent or *immobilier* Frank Partridge who had kept everyone else informed. The process had been drawn out because several parties had been interested in purchasing the place. The 17th century house which dominated the hillside village of St Servian had been in the same family for generations and had needed extensive renovation, but nevertheless was attractive to several French clients on account of its acreage of prime vines.

Evidently, there had been an internecine struggle behind the scenes but finally, there were just three contenders. The interested Parisian party dropped out first which left the Baileys versus a popular local French *domaine* owner who wanted to expand his wine empire. The drama was played out in the local press which unashamedly backed the French horse and caused a certain amount of anti-British feeling. Up in nearby Aniane, there had been the same sort of struggle when local wine growers were up against the Californian winemaking giant Robert Mondavi for some prime vineyards. The Yanks had been seen off thanks to the Communist Mayor who denounced the scheme as a capitalist plot designed to profit wealthy US investors rather than his villagers, and then promptly sold it to the veteran actor Gerard Depardieu who had taken a fancy to the land himself. There was still a legacy of bitterness over the fact that the mayor had seen off big business but had been beguiled by showbusiness rather than local business in the end.

The struggle in St Servian created unease amongst the ex-pats who were torn between not wanting to be unpopular, and the longing for some fascinating, glamorous fellow countrymen to land in their midst. They were to lose out on both counts.

At first there had even been a rumour that the couple in question might be Posh and Becks who were known to be looking for a place 'to chill' in the South of France. This had almost been too exciting for the troops and had given rise to many an exclamatory discussion. Sue, the tennis coach was beside herself but was rapidly deflated by the others. 'Don't be ridiculous, Sue,' growled Alan who couldn't think of anything worse. 'As if they'd come anywhere near us, even if it is them. They'd be surrounded by an entourage of bodyguards in track suits and ponytails who'd keep you well out', he added unkindly.

Frank had put them straight. 'It's not anyone you'll have heard of,' he reported. 'It's a man from Oldham who's made a fortune in computer mouse mats and now wants to get into the plastics industry out here.'

The thought was sobering and when Bill Bailey, or 'Mickey Mouse' as Lance then called him, won the day through sheer persistence and ever higher bids, there was no rejoicing in ex-pat land. Once he'd set his mind to something, he didn't give up easily, did Bill. To make matters worse, he then set about inflaming the locals still further by bringing out his own team of British builders to do the renovation instead of giving much needed employment to local firms. They in their turn then outraged everybody by never spending any money in the village, preferring to buy crates of beer and beefburgers from the *supermarché* which they noisily consumed every night in their campsite beside the house. 'Bloody fool,' commented Lance. 'We'll all pay for this.' And for once no-one contradicted him.

This, then, was the baggage that the Baileys arrived with, and the barbeque was the first opportunity everybody had to come face to face with the man and his much younger whey-faced wife. After all the build-up, the reality was disappointing, if predictable. Bill Bailey was a bluff northerner entirely used to getting his own way and who, as he boasted about himself incessantly, didn't suffer fools gladly – whether they be English or French ones.

Yes, he said, wearily, in response to intensive grilling from people like the Stanhopes who would infinitely have preferred a French grandee to take over the manor rather than a jumped-up mouse mat king, he had heard about the resentment that he had engendered in the area amongst the French, but he didn't give a monkey's. 'They're living in the Middle Ages, this lot,' he expounded. 'They'll remain that way too unless they've people like me around to give them a kick up the backside. I've got a lot of business interests in France now and I've got as much right to be here as anybody else – more, in fact.' He looked meaningfully at Rex Stanhope.

'What's more,' he warmed to his theme, 'I've got plans to make this region hum. There's a lot of potential here, only these jackasses don't make the most of it.'

'But, Bill, you can't just come here out of the blue and start rampaging around changing everything and riding roughshod over the locals – they'll hate you for it and you'll find it impossible to live here,' remonstrated Rex. 'Oh yes?' replied Bill 'And you're representative of the locals, I suppose, with your house in Chelsea and your fancy farmhouse here for when you feel like it (he had done his homework). I suppose you lot think that just because you go and 'soak in local colour' by sinking a *pastis* or two at the village bar and letting Pierre the plumber rip you off, that the

French are going to love you for it. Well, let me tell you, they despise you too, all of you, and since nothing's going to change that, you might as well do as you please. I certainly shall.'

After this, it was downhill all the way, socially, Jenny found. Nobody appeared to appease Bill, and his wife, Bryony, a thin colourless creature with rather dirty looking hair twisted into shopgirl braids, said very little, looked bored and yawned a lot. She was much younger than Bill, in her early thirties if that, Jenny guessed, and no doubt his third or fourth wife. Although, surely no wife stuck around for long. She seemed to be even more of a doormat than Jean, and that was saying something. Talking of which, where had Lance disappeared to? Not that she wanted him around, mind you. If anybody was going to stick in Bill's craw tonight it would be Lance, who could be even more bellicose than Bill.

After his little contretemps with Judith, Lance was in no mood for inane social chatter as expertly practised by most of the daft women at these gatherings – and not a few of the men. Nor did he fancy squaring up to Mickey Mouse just yet – though he relished the thought of a future encounter. Bloody little red-faced arriviste with his mousey wife – if she was his wife. Typical of the kind of people with money nowadays.

Ducking inside the house to avoid Jean's nitwit friend

Peggy approaching with the ghastly Bailey pair, he made for Alan's study where he knew the whisky was kept, and poured himself a slug.

Damn that woman, he thought, thinking of Judith. His heart was pumping uncomfortably and he knew his blood pressure had soared another few degrees. Just what was she bloody implying, and just what had she seen in Vevey? Looking at himself in the mirror above Alan's mantelpiece, from habit, he noted with annoyance and not a little alarm that he looked sweaty and dishevelled. If he were back in London, he would adjust his trademark bow tie at this point, but as it was his 'fun' Hawaiian shirt was sticking unattractively to his chest and his arms protruded fatly like hairy ginger logs from the too tight short sleeves.

Really, leisure clothes did not suit him, he allowed, not for the first time. He didn't look… well, he didn't look important enough to put it bluntly. After all, at his age with a fine career at the top of the advertising tree behind him, and a splendid one as an author and *eminence grise* on la belle France in front of him, he should, and deserved to, cut a dash. He must make a shopping trip to Montpellier soon and get some summer suits made up.

Sinking into one of Alan's faux-leather armchairs, he reproached himself – an unfamiliar response – with getting so angry with Judith so quickly. It looked bad. What was it about that woman that got up his nose so much? He had the impression that she was sneering at him, perhaps that was it. She was aloof and not easy to know, unlike the rest of the gang out here who were only too bloody easy to know. He felt as though she had got the measure of him and didn't admire what she saw. He could see that she had the kind of quick intelligence that could be a challenge to him, and he wasn't used to women challenging him.

Well, he'd show her. He too, had got the measure of her. She wasn't quite what she seemed, he was sure of that. Why had she given up teaching so young? She had something to hide – or if she didn't, she must have been born anxious. She looked like a frightened rabbit at times – the kind of rabbit Lance would like to squash under the heel of his boot. You could bet your bottom dollar she was a virgin too, which is why any hint of sexual activity was distasteful to her. Her mouth had actually puckered like a cat's bottom when she was talking about seeing him and Sophie. Silly cow.

And what of it, if he and Soph had been in a bit of a clinch. It wasn't as if he had done anything to encourage her. The girl was like a bitch on heat. Probably all those teenage hormones rioting. It was only natural that she wanted to experiment and found an older, wiser man like himself more alluring than the spotty young boobies of her own age who could only grunt by way of communication and wouldn't be able to afford to buy her a drink.

True, he wouldn't want Rex and Camilla knowing about his '*tendresse*' with their daughter, but dammit, the girl was old enough to look out for herself even if she was underage technically. He was looking forward to their planned dinner together before she went back to school. He would take her to a little place he knew by the beach where they weren't likely to be spotted by anyone. And after dinner, perhaps, a moonlit stroll along the beach…

Anticipated pleasure at the thought of this was interrupted by footsteps in the house and Jenny Knight calling him. Hurriedly he drained his whisky and left the study. More shaken than he cared to reflect on, he decided to head down to the local bar and find Roland, the elderly owner's son, a man of about his own age with whom he found he could converse easily in a mixture of French and English. Not only did they like drinking together when the going got tough at home, in Lance's case, but he had also discovered that Roland and he shared an interest in pubescent girls.

Roland had taken him into his living quarters above the bar one day some weeks back and shown him some magazines and a website on his computer that featured some very interesting material. He also said that he knew of a club in Montpellier where the two of them might go one day soon and explore the situation further.

Yes, thought, Lance. I'll head off to Roland's now for a nightcap. It's good to have at least one friend and ally in this kingdom of bloody fools.

'Just off to get a cigar at the bar,' he called to Jean on the way out. 'Don't wait up for me. I'll find my own way home.'

6

London

Campion and co. had its head office in Kensington Church Street, handily placed for expensive restaurants where Lance took his prospective clients for long, self-congratulatory lunches.

In the mid-90s his advertising and marketing company had probably reached its peak. Lance had capitalised on pitching for accounts that more principled companies wouldn't touch, and the clients were so indebted to him that they paid over the odds. Plus, Lance was smart. He knew his market and his charm, facility with words and general chutzpah won him accounts in the first place. After that, his snappy slogans and successful campaigns kept them coming back for more. Plus, of course, he knew his clients' weaknesses. And it was here that Lance emerged triumphant. He knew how to make a virtue of the less ethical aspects of a business so that, recently for example, he had successfully promoted an armaments fair in London; turned around the finances of a dodgy steroid manufacturer; and recruited hundreds of new members into a cult church where, in time-honoured fashion, vulnerable young people were parted from any money they had.

'Imagination, dear', that's what I've got, he explained to his increasingly tiresome wife Jean who didn't even try to understand what he did for a living. But she understood more than he thought. 'What Lance is really good at is marketing himself', she disloyally told her mother once – her mother, who couldn't fathom why her once beautiful and sought-after daughter was now shackled to a man who clearly bullied her and had now alienated their only child too. Sarah was just fifteen and had turned from a bright, enquiring, enthusiastic girl into a sullen, withdrawn, tearful soul who distressed her mother and angered her father.

But Lance had other things on his mind these days. He was hopeful of landing a really big fish – a publisher called Kevin Prince, who had a stranglehold on the young teen magazine market. Prince had eleven titles in all with oily names like Sweetpea and Spicechick and they absolutely raked it in.

What they were peddling, Lance found to his surprise, was sex. Even he, man of the world, had been astonished by the nakedly raunchy content of some of them. He had assumed, had he thought about it, they would be full of make-up tips and harmless gossip about boybands. What he found was porn dressed up as 'Health issues'. 'Why oral sex is good for you'; 'Yoga to make you orgasmic'; 'Sandwich anyone? Why threesomes are cool' were sample headlines.

Surely the parents of these 12-17 year old girl target audiences were unaware of what their little chicks were reading? But not for much longer, he thought. Already some concerned organisations like Family Comes First were causing problems for Kevin by speaking out in the media about the 'offensive, predatory, demeaning' material in such magazines, and Kevin was understandably rattled.

'What we need mate,' he said to Lance, over a splendid lunch in Launceston Place, 'is to have answers ready when we're attacked. I want you to prime our editors on how to cope with hostile enquiries. You know the sort of thing– how we're working to Department of Health guidelines to ensure young girls know how to take responsibility for themselves; how we actually promote safe sex, and then, 'course, only for those over the legal age; how we tackle serious issues that they're too afraid to discuss with parents and teachers and such like… I want our agony aunts to emerge as caring counsellors rather than sex-mad porn queens.

'But we're gonna have to be a bit more careful', he conceded. 'I'm gonna suggest that we start carrying more book reviews or something, so we can point to our unbeatable 'arts coverage". Here he gave a wheezy laugh and stubbed out his cigar. 'I take it we're on the same wavelength aren't we Lance old man? You should be able to put a more respectable spin on things? You're good with words. All this recent fuss is just a storm in a teacup I hope. Once it all dies down and parents forget to check their kids' reading matter, we'll be back in business. Come to think of it, they should be celebrating that their kids are reading anything – right?'

'Of course,' said Lance smoothly, thinking that priming some of the bird-brain editors he'd been introduced to in Kevin's office would be an uphill task. Perhaps he could hold up autocue cards for them if they went on air. He doubted whether many of them could pronounce 'responsibility' let alone know what it meant. 'Don't worry, Kevin. I know just how to handle this.'

Still, this would be a useful exercise for him, he thought. This world of teen magazines had confirmed for him something he had long thought: teenage girls are up for it, even those of ten or eleven. They were gagging for sex and the fact that they bought these magazines in their thousands just went to prove it. A nasty saying he had once heard came to mind: 'Old enough to bleed, old enough to butcher'. Just so.

In the past he had justified his interest in pubescent girls to himself by quoting the classical poets. Andrew Marvell for instance had fallen in love with the 15-year-old daughter of a friend of his and written about her without fear of condemnation in his poem 'Young Love'. In fact his poetry, and that of many others who were now deified as great poets, swarmed with references to tender shepherdesses and young nymphs. This, of course, was before the bloody nanny state and its crass laws governing the age of consent. Lance knew he sailed close to the wind, very close, in this day and age, and knew he had to be careful in pursuing his interests.

Only recently, he had had a scary brush with the law over that silly little tart, Louise, a schoolfriend of Sarah's. She'd been up for it all right but at the crucial moment had kicked up a terrible fuss and there'd been a discreet visit to his office by Mr Plod in the form of a plain clothes officer. Charges, thankfully, were not going to be pressed, but he was left in no doubt that if anything of this kind were reported again, there would be real trouble.

If he hadn't been so busy pursuing the Kevin Prince account, he'd have pointed out in his defence to the police the kind of material that these young girls liked to read, not to mention act upon. Really, the whole thing was ridiculous.

7

The main square of La Prairie resembled that of nearly every other medieval village for miles around. It was dominated by the church with its elegant wrought iron bell tower and clock that not only chimed every hour, but also chimed it five minutes before the hour. Judith had asked various people why this was so and only elicited the reply that it was the custom in the Languedoc for the church clocks to chime twice over, once, presumably to warn you that the hour approached, and once more to herald the actual arrival of the hour.

This was all very well and quaint, thought Judith, but not so charming for those who suffered from insomnia. At midnight the huge, creaky gong had only just come to the end of its seemingly interminable tolling, when it cranked up and delivered all over again. In England, she had read in local newspapers of long-standing feuds between those in the village who wanted the church bells to chime, and those who wanted them silenced, at least at night. She reckoned it would end in murder down one day down here.

Beside the church there was an area of pollarded trees and benches where the village elders gathered, tiny old men in flat caps who had lived in the same village all their lives and now had no need to speak to each other, having long ago said all there was to say. Across the small street was a patisserie for the daily baguette and a *Tabac.* The real focal point of the village, however, was the Café Le Square, a modest affair, with a bar and a few sticky tables inside, and a few more plastic tables outside under awnings.

When she first arrived, Judith had been too intimidated to go in and brave the stares. The bar was peopled every morning from 7am onwards by a surly group of locals known by Lance as the *pastis* and Gauloises crowd. All were men of an indeterminate age; all wore caps of some kind; all smoked, and all of them stared, menacingly, at anyone else who came in. They appeared to be fixtures, for whatever time of the day, Judith passed by on her way to get her bread, they were there. In time, she learned that the stares weren't so much menacing as curious, or not even that. 'People just do stare down here, Judith,' Alan told her when she mentioned it. 'They are peasants, literally, and no-one's taught them not to. Just as well they don't go on the London tube – they'd be beaten up. Also, you have to remember that most of them have lived here all their lives and it's only in the past few years that the place has opened up at all, not just to foreigners, but, worse, to Parisians and other northerners seeking the good life. And I can tell you that they detest the Parisians far, far more than you.'

After that, Judith would brave the occasional mid morning café crème whilst reading the local paper. At least,

I don't bring in the *Daily Mail* she thought. It was extraordinary how preoccupied the English were out here by events back home. Most of the English national papers could be bought in the bigger villages, and were, by the dozen.

Once, soon after she arrived in the village, she passed by to see Lance and some his cronies enjoying the set lunch there. 'Come and join us, Judith', cried Lance. 'You should be here – this is your local. You can have three decent courses and all the wine you can drink for just 12 Euros.' On the point of declining, not least because she had already eaten, Lance added, 'And come and meet Roland who runs this celebrated eaterie with his father.'

Roland was a dark swarthy man in his fifties who gave her a cursory handshake. After a few moments, he went back inside saying to Lance '*A bientôt*, Lance. See you later.' 'I come here to enjoy a jar with Roland in the evenings sometimes,' explained Lance. 'I think it's important to mix with the locals. Roland's all right, although his father, Jean-Baptiste, who owns the joint, is a curmudgeonly old sod. Apparently he was some kind of great war hero in the Resistance, except that now he seems to be resisting the English as well.'

'Was there much Resistance activity down in this area then?' asked Judith, interested. 'Oh quite a bit,' said Lance. 'Rumour has it that Jean-Baptiste, who must have been in his early twenties then was involved with a local group who tried to blow up part of the railway line between here and

Beziers when a German ammunition freight train was passing through. But they were betrayed by someone. He managed to escape, but all his friends were shot.

'The trouble with any resistance activity like that was that the reprisals were terrible. Apart from shooting the participants, the Germans would take it out on the families and indeed on the whole community. They had a very hard war down here. At one point, Roland, told me, the only source of protein they got was from the wild snails they collected. No wonder they're so fond of the bloody things.'

The day following the barbeque was surprising in a number of ways. The first surprise was that light was not streaming in through the shutters as it normally did. That could mean that a storm was about to break and bring some much needed rain. It also meant that Judith awoke much later than normal from an unusually heavy sleep, the kind where your legs feel welded to the bed. She lay without moving for at least twenty minutes thinking over the night before.

The second surprise was that as she mulled over Lance's reaction to her suggestion that he had been in Vevey with Sophie, she no longer felt any fear. Indeed, all the uncertainties and anxiety she had suffered over the last year appeared to have fallen away – and to have fallen away just when one would think they should have intensified.

It's as if, she thought to herself, I have spent the last year sensing that I had an enemy and yet not knowing the nature of him. Now, I know, only too well who my enemy is. It's true I don't know what he wants of me, or why, but I know something better than that. I know that he too has something to hide. He may scare me, but I, sure as hell, now scare him back.

This revelation of some kind of score settled revived her spirits and she hurried to dress, looking forward to settling down to work on her latest poem, a romantic epic this time in the style of one of Tennyson's Idylls of the King. Her own idyll wasn't to last for long, however. Her telephone rang, a source of pleasure for cheery souls, no doubt, but usually a harbinger of doom for solitary depressives like Judith who imagined, often rightly, that unexpected telephone calls spelt anything from annoyance to disaster.

This one was at the less catastrophic end of the scale but it was certainly irritating. Gillian Evans apologising to Judith for disturbing her Sunday, but – that correct supposition out of the way – could she possibly find the time to see Rose that day who was struggling with her Eng. Lit. revision and wanted to ask her about her Shakespeare set book. It wouldn't take long, Gillian promised. Only Rose was so grumpy at the moment and Gillian put it down to anxiety over her imminent exams. It would be just so helpful, knowing Judith had been a teacher, if she could spare her an hour later on.

Judith agreed reluctantly. She had hoped to put all that behind her but as soon as people knew you had taught, they felt they could make these kind of demands. Perhaps I should ask Gillian to come round for an hour to do my housework she thought malevolently. She had spoken to Rose briefly at the barbeque, feeling a bit sorry for her slouching around on her own. The girl was rather lumpen and shy and clearly hated being dragged around with her shrill, fussy mother and moronic father who aspired to part of the 'social whirl down here' as Gillian referred to it. Still, give me the girl rather than her mother any time, she thought. I'd better mug up on 'Romeo and Juliet' before she comes. With a pang she thought of the last time she had taught the play.

8

The summer term – that final summer term at The Chase over a year ago now – had started badly. The weather had been foul. Every morning, or so it seemed, one awoke to the tap-tap-tapping of light drizzle on the slate roof. Looking out of her bedroom window high up in the Victorian gothic building that had seen better days as the Railway Hotel in the prosperous Midlands spa town in which it stood, Judith thought the sky resembled one of the old grey woollen blankets still found on the sanatorium beds. She found it intolerable. In her waking dreams, she basked under an adamantine blue sky, so blue and cloudless that it hurt the eyes.

The girls were listless, the staff edgy and irritable. Every tennis match, every rounders fixture was cancelled or called off at half-time; every frippery of summer like the school fete or the sixth form garden party had to be indefinitely postponed. Only Veronica Templeton, with her indefatigable energy, seemed to be in high spirits, organising alternatives, suggesting changes, exclaiming, exhorting, demanding, whirling from one end of the school to the other down brown linoleum corridors, shiny with age, with her high-speed walk, clip board and brave smile.

Judith was transfixed by her. She was a one-woman laser show, a solo *son-et-lumière*. The previous term she had arrived out of the blue to replace the ailing Miss Bowen as headmistress of The Chase. Recently widowed, though only in her early fifties, she had arrived from Kenya where she had been much admired for turning around a once-marvellous girls school gone to seed. The governors of The Chase had been impressed by her get up and go and her enthusiasm for injecting new life into old (and lifeless, it was inferred) institutions.

The Chase Girls College was the kind of school at the end of the 19th century whose Principal had exhorted the young ladies in her charge 'to smile, bow and pass on' if they had the mischance to encounter any young gentleman in town. By the 1960s, Miss Bowen felt able to advise the girls to counter any mild compliment with: 'How very nice of you to say so,' before swiftly moving on – this, even whilst London rocked and the young coupled casually in public parks. By the millennium, all the school could usefully do was to instruct the nursing sister to hand out contraceptive advice and occasionally get the blushing young chaplain to give a talk on the importance of love in marriage.

The type of girl who boarded at The Chase came from the same kind of moneyed families who had always sent their offspring there. Only now their fathers were venture capitalists rather than squires, and their mothers were too busy sunning themselves abroad to sew on nametags. Whereas in Miss Bowen's heyday, the school had outperformed most similar institutions in academic performance, sending forth into the world a disproportionate number of doctors, dentists and vets, nowadays the school had steadily trickled down the league tables until one had to search for its name in the Top 500 rather than the top five.

Standards, in other words, had slipped, and the lacklustre atmosphere that now prevailed, meant that numbers were down and the waiting list was confined to eager Asians with brilliant mathematical abilities but poor linguistic and social skills, and the boorish offspring of Russian mafia who must have thought that an English education was just the thing for fledgling gunrunners. Veronica Templeton meant to change all that.

On an especially grey day, Judith calculated that she had now clocked up almost 16 years at The Chase. How many school assemblies, school dinners and school reports was that? It didn't bear thinking about. The last five years, she had been the Deputy Head thanks to her longevity of service. It was a career by default, and she knew it. In truth it had suited her independent and scholarly nature perfectly well. She had been able to pretty well coast through her days there, gaining pleasure from teaching those who were receptive, and largely ignoring those who weren't. There was not much pleasure to be had nowadays.

She had a few friends amongst her colleagues on the

staff but was always anxious to escape to her small flat within the main school building at the end of the day where she relaxed by cooking delicious meals for one and writing poetry. But the real bonus, of course, were the long holidays during which she happily explored France or Italy, and usually stayed for a while with her old university friend Jane and her husband Roger in a house they rented every year in the Languedoc not far from Montpellier. It was a contented life, if not a very stimulating or demanding one. But that, had she but known it, was about to change.

Judith's GCSE class that year were doing Romeo and Juliet for their set Shakespeare text. It was probably the easiest of the plays to teach to teenagers. Most of them could at least relate to a story of doomed young passion and they certainly enjoyed the idea of two rival gangs fighting in the streets. The other bonus was that there were two very good film versions of the play which were helpful to those who found the language difficult.

She had just finished teaching her English double lesson at the end of one Friday and was clearing her desk when Veronica tapped on the classroom door and walked in.

'Hello Veronica,' she smiled. 'What can I do for you?'

Relations between the two of them were friendly but formal, since Veronica's appointment there had been very little time to get to know each other socially. Veronica was an exceptionally striking woman, Judith thought now with her intelligent green eyes and quick mannerisms. She had already infused both staff and girls with a fresh sense of purpose and the governors were very hopeful that under her new regime things would improve.

Normally, she seemed totally in control; this evening, however, she looked exhausted and unsure of herself. 'Judith', she began, then faltered. She looked as though she might topple over. 'Veronica, are you all right?' asked Judith, looking concerned. 'You look absolutely done in.'

'I don't know what the matter is with me', admitted Veronica. 'Things are beginning to get on top of me, I think. There's so much to do here and so little time to do it and today I've had nothing but complaints about one thing and another – from parents, staff, girls and the chairman of the governors who is on my back night and day. Next thing I know, the cleaning ladies will walk out or the kitchen staff go on strike.' She smiled wanly, but Judith could see that she was close to tears.

'Poor you', said Judith. 'I'm sorry – look, if you're free now, we could talk about it… why don't I make you a cup of tea – or maybe something stronger?'

That was the start of their friendship. In Judith's flat during the next hour or two, Veronica, for what seemed like the first time in weeks, relaxed enough to confide in Judith about all the problems she was facing and how she was beginning to think that she might not be able to cope after all after such a promising start. A good listener, and a veteran of the school, Judith was able to offer useful advice and allay some of Veronica's fears. It was flattering to be confided in to such an extent and she found herself warming to this new Veronica who suddenly seemed so needy. Evidently Veronica too felt that she had gained a friend and ally. 'I'm so grateful to you, Judith', she said as she was leaving. 'I should have talked to you weeks ago instead of thinking I could shoulder all this on my own.' Briefly, she touched Judith's shoulder. 'Could we do this again sometime?' Of course, Judith told her, whenever you like.

After that there were many such meetings and Judith often found herself in Veronica's private wing at night after supper sharing a bottle of wine and talking over everything, not just school matters. She was delighted to be on such terms with someone she had considered rather remote and over-controlled. Veronica's now evident vulnerability touched her and to her surprise, she found herself confiding details of her own life – something she rarely did with anybody, even Jane.

'I feel a bit like Meursault, Camus's anti-hero in *L'Étranger*, she told Veronica one evening. 'Always the outsider, always detached in some way from my own life as well as everyone else's. I sometimes feel I walk through life on remote control, missing out on the deeper colours, the deeper sensations and invisible threads that draw everyone else towards positive, even dramatic action on occasion –

towards passion, I suppose.'

'Is that why you've never married?' Veronica asked quietly. 'Yes, I imagine so,' admitted Judith. 'I've just never felt strongly enough about anyone to do so. Again, it's like I've always been looking in at both myself and other people from outside, with interest sometimes, but hardly ever with any sense of engagement. I'm an observer, not an unhappy one, but perhaps a rather bemused one most of the time. I've certainly never been overwhelmed by passionate love for example. I've been too busy watching what I was feeling to actually feel it.'

'In a way, you're lucky,' replied Veronica. 'To love people is to suffer because there's always that risk of losing them. Love is dangerous all right, but you're only half alive if you're afraid to love. I've felt rather more alive lately.'

Looking back on it, it was this conversation, together with the way Veronica had been looking at her and the emotion in her voice that made Judith realise finally that Veronica was falling in love with her.

It was a curious revelation and one that she wasn't sure she could cope with. She knew of course that some women loved other women but she hadn't given it much thought. Now she wondered what a physical relationship with a woman might be like. Her experience of physical love with men had been limited and perfunctory. At university she had had a brief though unmemorable affair with a medical student; sex hadn't repelled her, but neither had it excited her. She knew when she went to bed with him that she wasn't feeling the right things, but she assumed it would get better. It was he who gave up on her first though telling her she was 'cold'. She hadn't had the experience or the energy to argue. Her friend Jane, with whom she discussed it, told her she just hadn't met the right man, and she accepted this. Somehow the experiment wasn't repeated.

Now, it occurred to her that she might have been barking up the wrong tree. Perhaps sex with another woman was the answer, although if that were so, it was odd it hadn't cropped up before. She'd had a half-hearted crush on a prefect at school but that didn't mean a thing. The Veronica business was puzzling though. She admired her and had become very fond of her. She could see objectively that Veronica was an attractive woman and now she was certain that Veronica desired her. If only she could reciprocate, perhaps she too would fall in love. In fact, knowing that Veronica desired her was in itself rather intoxicating; it meant that she now had to imagine what making love to her would be like and, to her surprise, she discovered that she would like to find out. With a small shudder of excitement, she decided that she would be receptive to any advance that Veronica might make.

She didn't have to wait long. Possibly sensing that Judith's attitude to her had changed, Veronica had taken her out to a small restaurant one Saturday night in a nearby village. Towards the end of dinner, they ordered brandies and Veronica had put her hand over Judith's on the table. 'I hope you know how much you mean to me', she murmured. Shortly afterwards, mellow with good food and a great deal of alcohol, they had returned together to Veronica's flat. As soon as they were inside, as Judith knew she would, Veronica took her face in her hands and kissed her, tentatively at first, but when Judith responded, with increasing passion.

The next morning, Judith awoke in Veronica's bed feeling as though she had been shot, so bad was her hangover. She lay still, not moving, trying to recall her seduction and remembering disappointingly little about it. Certainly, she thought, she had enjoyed the new sensations at the time and dimly she thought she remembered Veronica telling her she loved her. God, how was she going to face her this morning? One thing she knew for sure was that she didn't reciprocate the feelings Veronica had for her. Last night had been an experiment, that was all.

By the time she opened her eyes, Veronica was out of bed in the bathroom. When she returned the atmosphere was awkward. It being Sunday, they both had to attend morning church at the abbey in the town where the school held its services. They dressed quickly, not looking at each other or saying much before Judith left to tidy up in her own flat. Already she was experiencing her usual detachment from the situation. What had happened now seemed positively dreamlike. How could she have been so stupid as to allow all this to get so out of hand? It was totally inappropriate to have a sexual relationship in this setting. Veronica had been so silent and tense this morning that she guessed she was regretting it too. She sighed heavily, cursing herself. One thing she was sure of was that there would not be a repeat performance. This was the end of something, not the beginning.

9

After the bedroom-scene as Judith referred to it in her mind (not quite so romantic as the balcony scene in Romeo and Juliet, but a turning point, nevertheless), her relationship with Veronica changed for the worse. It was disappointing that there had been no epiphany between the sheets. The sex had been warm and comforting, an act borne of close friendship rather than passion on her part at least but she still felt very attached to Veronica and hoped that the two of them could continue their friendship.

Veronica, however, had behaved oddly, unable, it seemed, to look at her or talk to her properly. In the following week, they had been alone together only once when Judith sought her out in her study one afternoon. Judith had tried to be natural and affectionate, seeking only to reassure Veronica of her friendship. Veronica seemed tearful and distracted. 'I don't really want to talk about what happened,' she told Judith in a strangled voice. 'I think we both know that it won't happen again because I now realise that we want different things. I wish I knew what you wanted Judith, but I don't. I can see, however, that it's not me.'

'I'm so sorry, Veronica, I would love us to continue the way we were – to be friends,' blurted out Judith, knowing, even as she spoke, how inadequate those words were. That single word 'friends' which has tolled the death knell for countless hopeful lovers through the mists of time. She loves me and I don't reciprocate that love, she thought. How corny is that? And what does it say about me, yet again?

As she left, Veronica raised her head mutely and Judith could see that her eyes had tears in them.

She could not have predicted what happened next, and it happened with such speed that she had no time to reflect on whether it was fate or somehow malignly orchestrated. A sixth former had been sent to fetch a book from Judith's desk in her study whilst she was on a school outing. The girl, Camilla Reid, a stoat-faced troublemaker, had apparently 'found' some love poems that Judith had written for a new collection. Boldly, she had photocopied them and distributed them among some tittering friends as evidence that Miss Hay 'loved' Mrs Templeton.

Their many meetings and little outings had not gone unnoticed and the fact that Judith had been spotted leaving Mrs T's flat early one morning before breakfast solidified a good rumour. Parents were alerted who thought it less amusing than their daughters, other staff gossiped, and finally the governors were notified.

At the beginning of June, just before the end of the school term, Judith was called in to see the chairman of the governors, Charles Forres, a pugnacious little ex-naval commander who prided himself on running a tight ship, to account for herself. She had no idea what was coming:

'It has come to our attention,' he started, 'that a somewhat odd situation has developed – a relationship to be blunt, between yourself and the Head. I'm afraid some of the parents take a dim view.'

'What can you mean?' asked Judith, completely taken aback.

'I mean that some, how shall we put this, 'love poems' have been found in your possession which we have reason to believe were written to and about Mrs Templeton by you. She has confirmed this, saying only that you appear to have developed "some tender feelings" towards her this term which, unfortunately, have been noted by many of the pupils. Without wishing to put too fine a point on it, she intimated that an attempt at seduction had been made which she felt was totally inappropriate.

'But those poems were nothing to do with Veronica,' said Judith. 'They were written for my next collection – I'm a published poet. And as for any "feelings" between us, you must ask Veronica what the real situation is.'

'I realise this is an extremely delicate matter,' continued Sir Charles without giving any sign that he had heard her, 'but we, the governors, have put our total confidence in Mrs Templeton. We believe she is doing a splendid job here at

The Chase and we feel that this unfortunate incident cannot be allowed to interfere with the way we want the school to be run. I'm sorry to have to put it like this, but of course, we will have to consider your position here very seriously.'

Angry tears sprang to Judith's eyes. It was monstrous. She had been utterly betrayed by Veronica of all people. It was also, she saw, completely useless to argue. Her defence would not be listened to or required. She'd been tried and convicted in her absence. They wanted, indeed, needed, to believe this particular version of events.

'Don't bother to consider anything,' she cried. 'I resign here and now. I can see that there's no point in trying to put my side of the story.' Later, she couldn't remember leaving the room or finding her way, blurred with tears, back to her flat where she lay on her bed crying with anger and humiliation. Veronica, she was told, was conveniently away at a conference when she tried to find and confront her. Clearly, her job had been more important to Veronica than any personal feelings – certainly when they weren't really reciprocated. She had understood that her career was threatened and had decided that Judith must be sacrificed. In a way, Judith felt sorry for the woman. I wouldn't want to live with myself if I were her, she thought. Her betrayal had been breathtaking and damnable.

Within two days Judith had packed up and left The Chase whilst everybody was on leave. This had been planned beautifully she thought. Her mortification was complete and she spoke to nobody except her friend Jane in

London who told her to come and stay with her for as long as she liked while she considered her future plans. Thank god for Jane, thought Judith, though already she knew that London wasn't far enough away.

10

Ben lay in bed with his eyes closed. It was 7.00 am and he had to be at school by 8.00 am. He lay rigid with his fists clenched and thought of the day ahead.

He had attended the local secondary school in Vevey for a year now and it wasn't getting any better. When he and his mother had moved down to the south of France last year 'in search of better life' as Fern put it, she had assured him that he would much prefer school in France and that he would pick up the language easily. Wrong on both counts.

His comprehensive back in Bicester hadn't been great but he'd had good pals and had enjoyed all the practical lessons like carpentry and information technology. And he had played in the first football team who were absolutely ace and could beat the shit out of all other local teams. By contrast, French school was really horrible.

For a start, it was unbelievably regimented. He hadn't believed it at first when someone told him that there was a national curriculum in France which meant that every schoolchild is learning the same subject at exactly the same time all over the country, but it was true. And everything, he found, was run on almost military lines like that. The students sat in rows, head down, copying stuff from the board all day it seemed, and the teachers didn't teach, or discuss anything, they just lectured. And they had no relationship with the students at all. They hardly even knew their names.

Even worse, it was all just academic work all day. There were hardly any extra-curricular subjects like art or drama or music – all of which Ben enjoyed. And only a bit of physical education. If you wanted to play football you had to do it outside school hours by joining a local club. How sad was that?

But, of course, the very hardest thing for Ben was the language. He couldn't ever really speak to anybody, let alone make friends. French schools made no concessions to non-French speakers and you just had to get on with it. And it wasn't like his mother said. He couldn't just 'pick up' French because hardly anyone ever spoke to him. And when they did, it was to make fun of his halting French and foreign ways. It was OK for little kids. Apparently it was easy to learn a new language up until about ten years old, but Ben was now sixteen – fifteen when he arrived.

The work was so hard too, whether you were French or English. Non stop maths, French and science. Hardly any Geography and then only about French rivers, and History was a complete joke. No wonder the Frogs were so nationalistic – they only ever seemed to learn about that git Napoleon and all the battles they were supposed to have won.

He couldn't bear it. He really couldn't. And worse, he couldn't really talk to his mother about it. She had managed to make a go of it alone in France with him and he didn't want to let her down. His father had buggered off when he was twelve and after three miserable years living hand to mouth in Bicester, Fern had finally decided that if they were going to be poor, it would be better to be poor in the sunshine.

It had been a struggle at first nevertheless and they had lived for a couple of months in a caravan in the garden of Fern's neighbour's sister and her husband which was why they had come to this part of the Languedoc. Fern had never heard of it before. Now they had found a small house rent on the edge of Vevey and Fern had found a job she liked in an arts-and-craft shop in the old centre of town and started to make friends and feel more at home.

Ben loved his mother and being a sensitive soul, didn't want to make her life any more difficult than it was. She had had hopes of meeting a nice, rich man down in the South of France ('Well, there aren't any in Bicester are there?') but so far she hadn't had any luck. Both of them were lonely, if the truth be told. He, in particular, was extremely lonely and desperately missed his friends in England. Fern had promised they could go back at Christmas. But it was May, for god's sake. How could he last till then?

He lay now paralysed by the thought of another day, trying to fight back the tears that came now embarrassingly frequently, unbidden. At school, he would sometimes have to go and stand in the lavatories till the sobs stopped, emerging red-eyed but with no sense of relief. He squeezed his eyes tightly now to stop them, but if anyone had come into his room at that moment they would have noticed two trickles sliding down his cheeks and been alarmed for him.

Not far away that same day another lonely teenager was also almost in tears. Rose had just learned from Gillian that Judith had agreed to see her that afternoon to give her some coaching.

'How could you?' stormed Rose at her mother. 'I don't want coaching from some old bat here. It's my half term, or had you forgotten? It's bad enough having to be away from all my friends at home and being dragged to a million awful barbeques with you lot without your fixing up extra schoolwork this week behind my back.'

'Rose, you should be pleased,' said Gillian. 'Judith is a very nice English teacher and she'll be able to help you with that coursework on Romeo & Juliet that you're finding so difficult. Really, I thought I was doing you a favour. Besides, you've got nothing else to do today.' 'No, quite.' said Rose. 'That's my point. There is nothing else to do here but that doesn't mean I want to discuss Shakespeare with some boring old teacher. This is supposed to be a holiday from all that.'

Gillian despaired. The child was so unpleasant and sulky at the moment. Why couldn't she be more like that

Stanhope girl who managed to combine being a teenager with a certain degree of charm.

In stony silence, they set off for Judith's in the car after lunch with Rose clutching her heavily annotated edition of Romeo & Juliet and a few notes she'd scrawled on the coursework she'd been set. It never crossed her mind that the 'boring old teacher' was equally irritated at the thought of the coaching session to come and was quickly having a coffee and a cigarette in anticipation of a dull couple of hours with the sulky teenager she'd met briefly the night before.

Two hours or so later both Judith and Rose were surprisingly enjoying themselves. Both had realised that their first impressions of each other were mistaken and were now chatting like old friends. Judith had dealt with Rose's assignment – 'The course of true love never runs smooth'. Discuss this with reference to Shakespeare's play Romeo & Juliet. Your own experiences can be bought to bear on the subject too (optional).' – easily and efficiently. Rose thought she now properly understood Juliet's crucial balcony 'What's in a name?' speech and the subject had naturally lent itself to a more general discussion.

Judith was so helpful and so understanding that Rose found herself confiding in her all her problems about school and boyfriends and the fact that nobody understood her. Judith understood only too well. She herself had been there plus she had spent 22 years learning from and listening to young girls and she sympathised with Rose's lament that she couldn't get a boyfriend because she was too shy and awkward and didn't have the right figure – unlike Sophie Stanhope she added.

Judith then said something that startled Rose and made her think. 'I don't think Sophie's very happy either.'

'Why not? She's got a body to die for and all the boys buzzing around her like flies.'

'It's true she's an attractive girl,' admitted Judith, 'but, from my limited observations, I would say that she's just as insecure about herself as you are. Maybe she just disguises it better with all that showing off and bogus sophistication.'

Rose would have given anything at that moment for Sophie to hear Judith describe her adult ways as 'bogus sophistication'.

'I also think', continued Judith, rather indiscreetly, 'that she's a bit of a poor little rich girl. Her parents don't seem to notice her behaviour or care about what she's doing very much. I think a lot of what she does and says is attention-seeking because she doesn't get much notice taken of her by the people she wants to notice her.'

'That's probably true,' said Rose thoughtfully. 'I hadn't looked at it like that but you're right. I mean, my parents wouldn't let me hang around people like Lance Thingy in the way she does. Anyone can see that he's a dirty old man who's just lusting after her. She can't see that someone like that wouldn't be interested in her scintillating conversation alone. I couldn't believe it when she told me after that barbeque that she's going out to dinner with him – just the two of them – at the end of this week. I asked her if her parents would let her and she just said of course they would and that they probably wouldn't even ask her where she was going.'

'Yes, you're right,' said Judith, thinking that she mustn't let on just how horrifying she found that bit of information. 'You complain about your parents shepherding you around everywhere like a little girl, and fussing over you, but you wouldn't like it at all if they didn't care where you were or what you were up to. I think, by the way, she paused, selecting her words carefully, that you should try to dissuade Sophie from going out to dinner with Lance if you see her beforehand.'

'Oh, I've already tried,' said Rose, 'but she doesn't listen to me. She thinks I'm just a baby and that she's so smart going out with older men. Anyway, Sophie's nothing to me. I just wish I had some decent friends my own age around here, that's all. Mum's already told me that we're spending most of the summer holidays here too, worst luck. Will you still be here then?'

'I should think so,' smiled Judith. 'This is my home now. I'll tell you what, when you come back in the summer, I'll introduce you to a young friend of mine out here. You might get on well. He's a little older than you and called Ben. I occasionally give him lessons in French because he moved to Vevey with his mother last year and is still struggling with the language.'

'I'd like that,' said Rose. 'Thanks, Judith,' she added. 'May I call you that? You don't seem like a teacher at all. You've been really helpful.'

And so have you, thought Judith. But what I do with the nugget of information you've brought me, God only knows. I just don't think I can interfere. Lance gives me the creeps but he's friendly with those Stanhopes and it really is none of my business. Maybe he is only taking a fatherly interest in Sophie, but I doubt it.

She waved Rose off with Gillian. 'Take care, Rose,' she called, 'everything will be all right, you'll see.'

II

When Lance arrived rather breathless at Café Le Square the night of the barbeque, Roland could see at once that he was out of sorts.

'What is it, my friend? A girl has said no?'

'No, no, no,' said Lance, exasperated. 'Be a good chap, Roland, and get me….' He was going to say whisky so as to continue the way he had started, but then remembered that French bars only stock ridiculous export whisky with bogus names like Sir Edward's.

'I have just got in some especially good red wine,' interrupted Roland, reaching below the counter for a bottle. 'You will love it, Lance.' He kissed his fingers appreciatively. It is from Provence, very old, very good. A wine from Bandol – you have heard of it? Made from the Mourvèdre grape – very spicy, very good for you.'

Lance thought, not for the first time, that it was odd for a small, scruffy café cum restaurant in the sticks to buy in such decent wine. Roland had produced several magnificent bottles on different occasions. Sometimes Lance would buy a dozen off him. Roland knew how to charge for it and Lance supposed he made a small commission on it, but so far it had been well worth it. Now he swirled a little round in his glass sniffing it in the way his more wine-literate colleagues had done in the heady days of four-hour lunch breaks at Le Gavroche.

'This is excellent, Roland,' he pronounced. 'I feel better already.'

Practically all the restaurant's customers had gone for the night. Roland's father now appeared from the back, wiping his hands on a filthy apron. '*Bonsoir*, Jean-Baptiste,' called Lance genially, all thoughts of Judith now firmly on the back burner, '*comment ça va*?'

'*Eh Bien*,' growled Jean-Baptiste turning back into the kitchen. Grumpy bugger thought Lance, but you had to admire somebody like that, who had had such an appalling war and lost most of his friends in it. Roland had told him that he hadn't really been the same since the terrible shoot-out, not that he would know, since he hadn't been born then. Things hadn't improved apparently after Jean-Baptiste's wife had done a runner with the local butcher when Roland was about twelve. 'These things happen', shrugged Roland philosophically whilst relating this tale. 'The women in the village looked after us – better than my mother *en effet*.'

'Let's take this upstairs with us,' he now said, nodding at the bottle after his father had gone. 'I have some new things of interest to show you.'

Happily, Lance trotted after him up the dark, narrow staircase that led to Roland's bachelor quarters. It was really very good being friendly with the natives, he thought. He was rather privileged. Not many of his fellow countrymen had managed to integrate at all. Of course, most of the clots couldn't speak French well enough and were still bleating about not being able to find baked beans in the shops. He had heard of some villages, mostly in the Dordogne and Lot admittedly, where the English had organised local cricket teams. Why didn't they just stay in England, Lance wondered. They lived in France like bloody outlaws: they didn't get a *carte de sejour*, allowing them to stay in the country; they didn't make tax returns in France (well, neither did he to be fair); they never bothered to re-register their cars, even though it was a legal requirement after a year; they badgered the local *épicerie* to stock Marmite. They were hopelessly insular. He was surprised that they didn't try to drive on the left. He thought he was probably the only one of their number who had actually been invited inside a Frenchman's house.

He wondered now how the latest upstart to hit the area, Bill Bailey, would get on. 'Have you met the new Lord of the Manor yet?' he asked Roland who was downloading some pretty meaty stuff. 'I wouldn't shake his hand if you paid me', said Roland darkly. 'I have plans for him, my friend. He will not trouble us for long, I think.' Lance chuckled, wondering, not for the first time, if Roland was some kind of hit man on the side.

*

Jean Campion had no intention of waiting up for Lance. She knew well enough that he would return drunk and aggressive and try to pick a fight with her if she was still up. Wearily, she made herself a camomile tea and went upstairs to their room. If only she could at least have a separate bedroom, she thought. Over the years it had become increasingly impossible to get a good night's sleep with Lance snoring and coughing beside her, especially now that he drank so heavily.

Sex, thank god, was hardly ever on the agenda anymore. On the occasions it was, it was an entirely unilateral affair; she was not consulted, either before, during or afterwards. To think she had once been in love with the man and couldn't wait for him to hold her....

Everyone had told her she was making a mistake in leaping into marriage with Lance, especially her watchful parents who were alarmed that their much-loved only child was throwing herself into the lion's den. Lance had been dashing and amusing with his ironic drawl and worldly sophistication. He was also ten years older than she was and much, much more glamorous and interesting, she thought at eighteen, than the boys of her own age who fumbled with her unattractively and couldn't even afford the price of two cinema tickets. By contrast, Lance in his late twenties was already running his own PR & advertising business. A big man, his stockiness was offset by stunning pale blue eyes, regular features and longish thick fair hair – he resembled nothing so much as a proud young lion she used to think. His energy was intoxicating and there was something incredibly sexy about his self-belief. He was also, as her father gently tried to point out, narcissistic and carelessly cruel.

Even before they married, Lance would laugh at her opinions and ideas. 'What do you know, sugar lump?' he would say. 'Leave the thinking to me'. And she would laugh with him, thinking what a relief it was in a way to surrender even her thoughts to this charming, clever man. If Lance had told her the world was flat she would have believed him. And if he did go too far and humiliate her in front of his friends so that she was close to tears, he would make it up to her later, catching her round the waist and nuzzling her ear. 'Sorry, sugar,' he would say. 'You know you're my favourite little girl, don't you? I wouldn't hurt you for the world.' But he did hurt her, Jean reflected now, and had gone on doing so.

The worst of it had been his treatment of their daughter, Sarah. It had been fine until she was around thirteen and a sunny, sweet-natured child. But at the onset of puberty, the self possessed little girl who had never given them any trouble and was the mirror image of her patient, sweet-natured mother became moody, detached and difficult. With Jean, she was still amenable though withdrawn; but when her father claimed her attention or reprimanded her for her lack of motivation, her face clouded over and she usually stormed from the room. Lance's reaction had been anger and he would shout and rage at both of them. Jean had tried to point out that most adolescents go through a bad patch, but he wasn't interested in what most people did. 'She can go to hell', he stormed. 'I'm not paying through the nose for that little bitch to go to private schools. She's learning nothing except how to be unpleasant.'

And so it was that Sarah at sixteen failed most of her exams and left her academic London day school in disgrace. Jean made sure that she enrolled at a local sixth-form college but shortly afterwards, she left home and went to share a scruffy flat with people her parents didn't know and wouldn't want to have known. Lance disowned her entirely whilst Jean desperately set up hurried meetings with her in anonymous Oxford Street chain cafes and tried to persuade her to come home. She got by, she told Jean, on social security and was perfectly happy. She had no intention of coming home. She was sorry, she added, but it was better for everybody this way.

After a few months of this, she changed the phone number Jean had been able to reach her on and after that all contact was lost. Jean would pace up and down wet London streets looking for her in places she had seen her in the past but to no avail. Ignoring Lance's advice to forget her, she went to the police with photographs but when they heard the story, they told her there was little they could do. Sarah was by now seventeen. She had left home of her own accord. There was no reason to think she had been harmed in any way.

'It happens all the time, love', a nice policeman finally

told a shaking, weeping Jean. 'These youngsters want to forge their own way without us, I'm afraid. But they don't think of those who brought them up, do they? Your Sarah will most likely be fine. One day, she might come back and say sorry for the pain she's caused, you'll see. You sit there, and I'll get you a nice cup of tea.'

But by the time he came back, Jean had gone and was sobbing openly on a nearby park bench. She knew she had lost her only child and back at the station, so did the kind copper. He saw it only too often. It affected him every time. No use pretending it didn't.

That night, as every night, Jean thought about Sarah and wondered where she was – indeed, who she was now. She would be 24, she might even have children of her own. The pain never went away but it had dulled to the point where she could carry on and think of other things most of the time after eight years.

After the police station episode, Jean had resolved not to mention Sarah again to Lance. His attitude was inexplicable. He had never expressed any regret or shown his unhappy wife any support in her evident distress. It was the way he operated.

When three years ago, he decided to take early retirement and move to France, she had been pleased. She desperately needed a change of scene and she had long ago given up hoping that one day she would hear Sarah's key in the door. And, in fact, life had improved considerably. Lance was preoccupied now with writing his books and she herself had settled down to a far from unpleasant life in the sun, trying to create a beautiful garden out of an acre of dry scrub. They had a busy social life and whilst she hadn't found a real friend, she was never short of company when she wanted it. As for life with Lance – well, it was just life with Lance. They co-habited. She supposed they always would. She long ago stopped feeling sorry for herself that she had chosen the wrong man.

Lately, though, something more specific was bothering her. Generally, she never went into Lance's study where he worked on his computer – he had specifically asked her not to go in there for fear of disturbing all his papers, but one afternoon recently when he was out she had gone in to look for a map of the area that she thought must be in there.

She looked around her at the mess everywhere. Papers all over the desk, papers on the floor. But Lance had forbidden her to let the cleaner in. It was strange even being in here – in Mission Control as he called it. She looked on the shelves for the maps but they weren't there. Idly, she opened random drawers not really expecting to find them at all. The edge of a photograph under some other stuff poked out. Curiously, she pulled it out and looked at it. It was an old photograph of Sarah and her then best friend Louise. They must have been around 15 and they were on a beach sunbathing topless. She remembered the holiday. It had been in Portugal and was possibly the last happy family holiday they had. Sarah had wanted to bring Louise with her and Jean had agreed.

The beach they went to most days was almost deserted and the girls thought they looked more like movie stars at Cannes if they took their bikini tops off. It was a strange photograph for Lance to have kept though. There were many photographs, much better ones, of Sarah by herself. Jean stared at it; it bothered her. It bothered her a lot. She didn't even remember taking it. Lance must have done.

Then at the barbeque tonight, that conversation with Judith. Why did Lance want her to confirm that he had been gardening with her that day? When, in fact, he had only helped her for about ten minutes. She could see that Lance had been angry – she knew all about that controlled fury. She could also see that Judith was shaken. She resolved to go and see Judith when she could. She liked what she knew of her – which wasn't much as Judith kept herself a bit apart from the others. But she felt she would like to know her better and she very much wanted to find out what Judith had said to Lance to make him that agitated.

12

Lance had carefully orchestrated his dinner alone with Sophie at the end of her half term. He told Sophie in advance that there was an excellent bric-a-brac market on at the weekend in the old port of Marseillan on the coast and that he would be motoring down in the afternoon to see if he could pick up some odds and ends at knock-down prices. He had pretty well furnished his house in this way and rather prided himself on the way he was able to haggle with the traders in passable French. Carelessly, he mentioned that there were plenty of clothes stalls and, as anticipated, Sophie was immediately hooked.

'Lance, you've got to take me,' she begged. 'I adore markets – I've got a really good eye for bargains, and I so don't want to go with mummy and daddy for the weekend to some old bores they know down near Carcassonne. If you told them you were looking after me for the day, I'm sure they'll agree to go without me. You can drop me back at the house afterwards and they'll be coming back Sunday morning anyway to pack up.'

This was music to Lance's ears. On a roll, he now took a gamble: 'What about bringing that friend along with you?'

'What friend?' asked Sophie crossly.

'The Evans girl – Rose, isn't it?'

Sophie tossed her hair indignantly. 'God no, Lance. She's not my friend – she just happens to be my age. She wouldn't be allowed out anyway, and she certainly wouldn't be able to pick out all the designer items which I'm sure I'll find lurking amongst the rubbish. Poor old Rose has pretty sad taste in clothes. Did you notice those jeans she had on the other night?' Sophie giggled unkindly at the memory. 'They were like totally the wrong shape and she had them hitched right up to her waist!'

'Well, if you're sure you won't be lonely with just me,' purred Lance.

'Course not, I like being with you. And you like being with me, don't you?' Sophie looked at Lance under her eyes the way she had practised in the mirror, Diana-style, and pouted. She mustn't let on how mega-excited she was about this trip. She had read in Cosmo about the power of the older man and whilst it was true she hadn't really liked the way Lance tried to poke his tongue in her mouth, she thought it wasn't any worse than what those poxy little public school boys did to her at every party she went to in London. At the Feathers Ball last year she'd had two of them pawing her all over at the same time. And then some. Lance, in any case, was so much more cool than them. For starters he was famous; secondly, he had money – money that she hoped he might spend on her; thirdly, he was definitely somebody to boast about at school. He was even good looking in an oldish, rumpled kind of way. He might take her to some swanky restaurant after the market if she played her cards right. God, come to think of it, what was she going to wear?

The weather was perfect on Saturday – just the job for the open top Citroen that Lance had just bought. As anticipated, he had easily squared the outing with Rex and Camilla who were delighted that he was taking a fatherly interest in Sophie and only too pleased to leave her behind at the weekend on the grounds that she'd be bored stiff at their house party. They hadn't had much option but to bring her out with them for half term but both were too busy socialising and refurbishing their French house to give much thought to their daughter or her needs.

'Benign neglect' works best for us, laughed Camilla when people asked her how she had coped with all her children as well as her endless travelling, charity lunches and new schemes for this and that. Sophie was the youngest by far of their five children and the only girl – a bit of a mistake really – as Camilla confided to her friends at the time. In fact, what Camilla meant was more like a bit of a bore. Soph was certainly going to screw up her plans for jetting around once the other four were off her hands.

In her time, god knew, she'd been a yummy mummy, always one of the first at their prep school, and later at public school to suggest and implement children's outings, children's parties, tennis tournaments, cricket matches, children's happenings generally. Her range rover was always crammed with her own and other people's kids, always off to some fun thing or other. Nothing was too much trouble. Their house in Oxfordshire was large enough to accommodate them all and there was always a nanny or two to help. And then the boys were so much easier in the way that they entertained themselves and each other and didn't get into hissy fits the whole time like girls did.

Camilla had been bewildered by Sophie growing up – the tears, the tantrums, the fallings out with friends, the whining, and now the boyfriend thing, though, it had to be said, Soph had gone quiet on that front. Why couldn't she just run around the garden like the boys did to let off steam? Camilla herself had been sporty as a teenager and holidays were full of bracing outdoor activities, most of them centred around the Pony Club. But Soph didn't want to ride or go swimming or play tennis it seemed. She really couldn't understand her at all, especially lately. Fine around other people when they were out, but mooching around at home endlessly looking at herself in the mirror and obsessing about clothes and make up and faddy diets.

What her mother didn't know and wouldn't have known what to make of them if she had, was that if one looked closely along the tender white skin inside Sophie's arms and thighs that one could discern numerous scars, some old, some newer and more liverish and one or two which hadn't yet healed.

*

Sophie felt pure pleasure as she and Lance whirled through bright acres of vineyards and sleepy little villages in his open top car on Saturday afternoon. Much thought had gone into her outfit. Finally she settled for her tightest jeans which rested just on her hipbones displaying a washboard stomach adorned by the obligatory jewel in her bellybutton. Her top, in fuscia pink had the words 'Ask Me' written over her breasts so that their curve distorted the letters but not their meaning. A wide-brimmed straw hat completed the outfit over which Sophie had tied a chiffon scarf which tied under her chin which held the hat in place and gave her what she thought of an Isadora Duncan look. Black Rayban sunglasses completed the cool image.

Lance had been appreciative. 'What a sexy little minx you are', he said when he saw her, and meant it. My God, he thought, they talk about predatory men but these young girls are crying out for it. They dressed like hookers. He would get lucky, tonight, he was sure of it.

13

Having fought so hard to secure his chateau in France, Bill Bailey, the computer mat king, was not a happy bunny. Two months had gone by since he had taken up residence and he had not managed to whip the French into shape in the way he had hoped.

Running anything, from a business, an estate, or even a car was proving a great deal more difficult than he anticipated. French bureaucrats, celebrated throughout the globe for being more numerous and more intractable than in any other country, were determined to stop Bill Bailey in his tracks, he informed anyone who would listen. It was a scandal, for example, he told the hapless Frank Partridge, whom he ran into in Vevey one day, that he hadn't been allowed to pay his local property taxes with a UK cheque book in the Mairie.

'But they only accept Euros,' Frank had reasonably pointed out.

'That's my point,' railed Bill. '*we* haven't joined the euro – they're so bloody inflexible.' Frank had to laugh. If anybody could outrank famously inflexible French megalomaniacs such as Charlemagne or Napoleon, it was

Bill Bailey. He probably had been a Frenchman in a previous existence.

Still Bill wasn't to be defeated – not by a long chalk. Strangely resistant to endearing himself to anybody, he set about antagonising everybody. His next target was unwise, however. Priding himself on being a bit of a gourmet, he had sampled many of the local restaurants and found them wanting. Yes, a good dinner could be had if you were prepared to travel to Montpellier or even Beziers, but what Bill required was a local place 'to get something decent to eat' as he put it at lunchtime. His wife Bryony was evidently lacking in the domestic department.

With this in mind he set about trying to buy Café Le Square. His own village, St Servian, only had a tiny bar which apparently operated out of someone's front room and La Prairie was the nearest place where you could have lunch. Café Le Square, however, was not to his liking. For a start he didn't like sitting on a grubby white plastic chair. Secondly, he detested the surly Roland and that revolting old peasant who hung around behind the bar chewing the cud with similar old relics. Thirdly, the grub was diabolical. 'Call this a bloody menu?' he'd asked the first time he was presented with the '*formule*' or set lunch. 'There's no damn choice'.

Bryony looked indifferent. She had quickly latched on to the *pastis* habit and didn't really give a toss about the food. When Bill was working, she went off to a bar in another nearby village where she'd discovered a younger, more interesting gang of mostly English and American dropouts who spent much of the day making the most of the cheap drinks and cigarettes. None of them were employed it seemed but they all enthused about the generous benefits they were eligible for in France. Often they passed joints around and Bryony felt more at home with them than with that boring, bourgeois crowd they'd met when they first arrived. She didn't let on to them that she lived in a sort of chateau – she thought they might burgle it if she ever invited them back there. Besides, she would certainly lose her street cred.

Unlike Bill, she rather liked it in France. It was cool. If Bill wanted to bugger off back to Oldham, she thought she might stay on. She rather hoped he would in fact. The novelty of being married to a rich man had begun to wear off. OK, so he rescued her from a lifetime of drudgery in Oldham when his eye had alighted on her in the typing pool of one of his companies a couple of years back, but the life didn't really suit her she found. And Bill had turned out to be a huge pain in the neck too, especially out here, bellyaching all the time about all the things he didn't like. She had preferred him being a big fish in Oldham and letting her enjoy what he called 'the fruits of my labours'. She missed the nights out with the girls where they would spend a fortune (Bill's fortune) on cocktails in Oldham's poshest wine bar followed by a night on the tiles. But, now that she was here and had made some new friends, she could scent fresh possibilities. And she had her eye on an

English lad she had met who had been one of Bill's building team renovating the house and had also decided to stay on in the sun. He was always down at the bar now and had found himself a room in a house nearby. She'd had to swear him to secrecy about the chateau.

And so Bill set about badgering Roland and Jean-Baptiste to sell him their café. What he had in mind was a more upmarket brasserie where you could get a decent steak. Frank Partridge had put the idea in his head by mentioning that the Chabots were thinking of selling up and moving down to the coast where they had cousins, but it turned out only to be the vaguest of plans and when Bill made his move, Jean-Baptiste was outraged.

'How could we possibly sell to an Englishman?' he raged at Roland who was equally indignant but tempted nevertheless by the staggering offers of money Bill had bandied about. 'We would be the laughing stock of all our friends… we could never recover. And what about the village? It would be an affront to the honour of France.'

'And just think of the food they would serve', was another refrain once the preposterous notion had spread to the diehards who nursed their coffees at the bar all day. 'It would be disaster. Nobody could eat here anymore. There would be nowhere to drink a coffee or a *pastis* first thing in the morning.'

Feelings ran so high that soon the entire village was up in arms. Bad enough to have so many 'Rosbifs' living in their midst, but setting up their own restaurant where they would serve jelly all day was unthinkable. Lance had been puzzled by Roland's reference to jelly when this had been discussed in his hearing. It was apparently an unshakable French belief in these parts that the English had an enormous appetite for jelly. Whenever this was mentioned it was greeted with whoops of derisive laughter. No amount of explaining that jelly was something that was only ever occasionally served at children's tea parties in England could convince them that jelly would not feature prominently on any English restaurant menu.

Whilst these discussions were on-going, Judith, who was as appalled as the local French that Bill Bailey might take over the café, began to notice anti-British graffiti appearing on village walls. Someone had even fly-posted the village warning of an 'English invasion'. It was the Hundred Years War all over again, she thought. It made her very uncomfortable and furious with the blundering Bill Bailey.

'That man has brought us all into disrepute', she complained to the Knights who were equally alarmed. Suddenly, the atmosphere of peaceful co-habitation looked like it was breaking down. Many of the English, even those who had been there for years, complained that people were snubbing them in the shops or the street. Even Lance couldn't calm things down. Roland had cordially explained to him that whilst Lance was his *bon ami*, he and his neighbours couldn't, in general, stand the English, especially those who thought they could come and take over French restaurants.

Finally, Bill retired defeated but defiant. 'I'll start a new restaurant next door if I have to,' he rallied. But, in truth, he was feeling pretty fed up with the way everything was going. He wondered if he would have been better off in Spain. At least they wouldn't want to re-fight the Battle of Agincourt the whole time. It was scandalous, the French attitude to the Brits. Who was it, pray, who had rescued the buggers not once, but twice, from the Hun? They could damn well keep France next time, he thought.

14

Gerald Thornton was one of life's disappointed romantics; that is to say he was a cynic, and people who didn't know him that well were often offended by his sharp tongue and critical manner. He was 52, his wife had died ten years previously from breast cancer, and he had on a whim sold up in England where he had been an independent publisher and moved to France where, with great difficulty but a kind of grim determination, had eventually set up an English bookshop near the top of a steep stone-clad alleyway in the heart of Montpellier's historic quarter. For the first five years he struggled to make ends meet. Books were expensive to buy, especially when imported, and his English clientele were largely reluctant to purchase – especially when their paperbacks cost almost a third as much again as they did at home. But gradually, by using his imagination and gritting his teeth, he came to be indispensable to that small section of a foreign population that needs or wants books in its native tongue and to the tiny fraction of the indigenous population which wants to, or has to, learn English. And, by diversifying into videos, greetings cards and cups of tea served outside on the pavement, Gerald was able to get by doing something he enjoyed in a city he had come to love.

Much thought had gone into the naming of the shop. When he arrived in Montpellier Gerald was an angry man. His wife had arbitrarily been taken from him; his business at home was at a standstill; he had nothing and nobody to lose by his move to France. Life was a bitch. Literature was the only refuge. His bookshop was to be his baby; naming her was not to be taken lightly. Not for him Ye Olde English Bookshoppe or even The English Bookshop. Nightly, when he couldn't sleep he ran through his literary lexicon: Shakespeare was clearly a possibility. 'The Tempest' appealed but people might think he was selling rain hats. 'A Tale of Two Cities'? Now that was quite apt but it was one of Dickens's lesser known works and it was associated rather strongly with Paris. 'Bleak House' was too depressing; 'Great Expectations' was too hopeful. 'Sense and Sensibility' might be taken for a therapy centre; 'Vanity Fair' for a beauty parlour. Suddenly it came to him: 'Wuthering Heights'. He was, after all, near the top of a hill and the Mistral wind did whistle down the alleyway in October. He was, too, he liked to think, a Heathcliffe figure, solitary, manly, misunderstood.

And so it was that the Wuthering Heights English Bookshop was born. It mystified the French postman but it appealed on the whole to the English exiles who felt it personified an English port in a storm with its union jack flag outside, its Penguin Classics and its Twinings teabags.

And an astonishing number of exiles there seemed to be in Montpellier, judging from those who found their way through the maze of medieval lanes to Wuthering Heights. True, many of them were only tourists passing through who had forgotten to buy a paperback at the airport and needed something to read on the beach or back at the hotel. But quickly Gerald got the sense of a very large resident English-speaking population, many of them American, who began to use his bookshop as a valuable resource, ordering books that they needed for work or pleasure which Gerald could usually get hold of within a week, and picking Gerald's brains (which were considerable) for suggestions.

Unusually, for an English bookshop in a foreign country, Gerald chose not to pander exclusively to the easy sales of 'bumpy cover' paperbacks – those whose contents were as lurid as the raised gold and silver and scarlet lettering on their covers. Of course they were available – they were his lifeblood pretty well – but he preferred to stock books of all kinds that he himself would like to read. Otherwise, where was the joy in the job? One might as well have been flogging shoes. So, crammed into every corner of the two floors of his small shop, were books of every kind: the classics, modern fiction, biography, history, art, language, science, film, poetry – you name it.

And sitting just to the right of the door on to the street was Gerald himself, virtually hemmed in by towers of books both on and under his desk either cursing at his computer screen as he wrestled with orders and invoices, or owlishly inspecting customers he didn't trust not to make off with a book without paying. Or, since he'd had the most expensive books electronically alarmed, watching them closely to see if they showed any signs of rendering the books they perused, without any intention of buying, unsellable by rough handling. At this, Gerald would invoke his inner child whom he had fondly named Ged, a diminutive of 'Gerald' and the name of a drummer he had once admired. Ged was merciless with these customers and what's more Ged had a hammer which he fingered meaningfully when he spied them putting them sticky fingerprints on photographic plates and bending back the pages so far that it broke their spines. If this happened, Ged would spring out and rain hammer blows on their heads. As they went down, he would stand over them waving the hammer in one hand and the broken book in the other. 'See how you like it,' he would scream, as their vertebrae splintered into a thousand pieces. 'Not so funny, is it?'

Ged, up until now, had had to be kept in harness in Gerald's imagination. When careless customers had actually broken the spines of new books or spilled coffee over them from a takeaway cup they were carrying, Gerald had managed to conceal his murderous impulses and merely suggested that they might like to pay for the books in question. Some did, full of apology. Some didn't and just walked out. There wasn't much he could do about it.

*

Apart from awkward customers, there was another potential enemy – local authors. In and around Montpellier there were dozens of both established and aspiring writers and Gerald would always try to promote them if he felt they were worthwhile, inviting some of them in to sign their books when they first came out. Indeed, there were many local authors who had reason to be grateful to Gerald for promoting their books vigorously by means of window displays or inviting them to exhibit at his stall at the yearly Montpellier book fair.

However, there were those whom Gerald would take against, either because he disliked them personally, or because he thought their books were rubbish. The worst of them were the ruthless self-promoters who felt that if they had written something, even if it was self-published as some were, Gerald was under an obligation to give them free publicity. Two years ago, Lance Campion had fallen firmly into this category. It wasn't his book, *Languedoc: The Four Seasons* which Gerald objected to. It was perfectly competent, even though Gerald was growing increasingly tired of French Dream books. It was Lance himself, who from the moment he swaggered into the shop bearing proof copies, got right up Gerald's nose. Everything about his manner, bearing and self assurance antagonised him. He knew before Lance strode up to his desk and interrupted a customer who was paying for a book that he would be coming to ask special favours of him in the full expectation of getting them. He knew who he was because he'd seen him around but he hadn't spoken to him before. And sure enough, Lance had virtually demanded that Gerald put on a special window display of his book when it came out, and had even, breathtakingly, in Gerald's view, written a glowing review of his own book which he suggested Gerald use in his monthly online newsletter.

Gerald had glanced at the proposed cover which featured the usual romantic shot of misty vineyards at dawn with a chateau in the background. 'Don't think much of the cover', he said. And before Lance could retort that he hadn't designed it, turned his attention to the press release Lance had written describing himself as 'an accomplished and sensitive chronicler of this beautiful and neglected region of France'. Gerald snorted. 'I take it that you are the accomplished and sensitive author of this touching tribute'? he asked. For a second, but only a second, Lance looked a little abashed. Recovering, he said defensively, 'Of course. Somebody has to do the pre-publicity. I can't trust the publishers to do anything. And the real reviews will come out too late for this month's newsletter and the book will already be in the shops by the time the next one appears.'

Gerald looked amused. 'Oh, and it wouldn't do to wait for the 'real' ones I suppose?' Lance bridled. 'Look, if you're going to be offensive, I won't bother you any longer. I was going to offer to come in and sign copies….'

'That won't be necessary', said Gerald firmly.

'I'd have thought a local bookseller would be glad to help local authors', retorted Lance. 'It's not as if you're exactly rushed off your feet here,' he added maliciously, looking round the empty shop. Gerald longed to release Ged and let him rain blows with his hammer on Lance's mekon-style head watching as the red blood soaked through that luxurious thatch of blond hair – (another source of irritation to Gerald whose own thatch was somewhat threadbare). Instead, he said merely: 'I help local authors I respect. That's my prerogative. I shall read your book and I shall stock it if I like the look of it and if I think it will sell. However, I'm certainly not going to give you any personal publicity. You're more than capable of publicising yourself and I'm doing you a favour by not letting you come here to sign books. If any of the customers actually met you, they wouldn't want to buy one.'

15

Judith had discovered Wuthering Heights by chance soon after she arrived in France and had been delighted with it. She had bought several novels and one or two books on the region and noted with interest the shop's courteous but taciturn owner, a well-built man, she guessed in his fifties, with thinning hair, clothes that looked untended though clean, and an intelligent face. She had never spoken to him but had covertly watched him as he talked to a man he evidently knew who was enquiring about a biography. He obviously knew what he was talking about and she liked the timbre of his voice. But she was glad he hadn't talked to her; she didn't need any help with her choices and he looked as though he could be difficult with anyone he didn't know. Besides, she was still too raw to field the inevitable questions about what she was doing in France. Not that this man looked like one for idle chatter.

Since that first time, she had been in several times. She enjoyed a day out in Montpellier, exploring its maze of small streets and squares with 17th- and 18th-century mansions as well as its astonishing new quarter, Antigone, a self-contained utopian development of shops, restaurants and housing beside the River Lez designed in neo-classical style by a Catalan architect Ricard Bofill (or Signor Paella as she had heard Lance refer to him).

Whenever she went into Wuthering Heights, Gerald, as she had discovered the owner was called, acknowledged her politely but made no conversational moves, so she was surprised to find him beside her suddenly when she had gone downstairs to browse through the well-stocked poetry section. There she had, to her surprise and pleasure, found two of her own Howard Hill collections, one of which she was looking at when Gerald spoke: 'If you're interested in poetry, I have another section upstairs for the classic poets, or are you happy here with the contemporary ones?'

Judith started, feeling guilty to be caught reading her own book, but of course he wasn't to know that.

'Oh, I'm fine, thanks. I've got most of the classic anthologies I want. But I like to see what the contemporary poets are doing.'

'Me too', said Gerald. 'There's quite a few local poets in amongst that lot – this area seems to attract them. Whenever I've time, I organise poetry readings here. You'd be surprised how many people show up… he's good, isn't he?' he nodded at the Howard Hill she was holding. Judith felt herself blushing like a schoolgirl. 'Mmm', she managed. 'Do you think so?'

'Yes, I like his stuff very much,' said Gerald. 'I think there are three collections now but I've only got two in at the moment. He appeals to me because he addresses the particular rather than the general. I appreciate his observations on the minutiae of life rather than the grand themes beloved by so many male poets. It seems to me that he almost writes from a woman's point of view, especially about love. I once tried to get hold of him for a big poetry event through his publishers, but they weren't having any of it. Apparently the guy's a bit of a recluse. I looked him up on the internet but he's never even given an interview.'

Judith couldn't look at him. She swallowed and said, huskily. 'I think quite a few writers shy away from media attention. Once they are in the public domain, they become creatures of the public somehow. Not just their writing, which everyone feels they can then pick over with reference to the person they now 'know' – you know the kind of thing. Oh yes, he writes like that because his mother abandoned him as a baby, etc., but their personal life too. I think it must be intolerable.'

Gerald looked at her carefully. 'You're right', he said. 'Proper, private people don't want public attention. They're right to shun it.' He smiled at Judith. 'If you want to come to our next poetry reading, it would be good to see you. I've got the details upstairs.'

Almost a year to the day since Tim Lavery had sealed his death warrant on the *Tribune* he found himself in Montpellier looking for a shady spot in which to have a beer. It wasn't a city he knew at all but what he had seen of it so far pleased him very much.

He had borrowed his sister's car and driven in from the

house they had taken for the summer, about an hour north of the city, anxious to flee from from the noisy demands of his young nephews who thought that Tim's role in life was to be canon-balled repeatedly in the pool. Tim's plan to get on with his novel whilst spending a month with Freya and James and their two sons had not worked out that well. Not only were his avuncular duties required at all times, but he was getting very bored with the smug married couple thing that his bossy older sister Freya did so well with her husband James.

Having done so well themselves, they now apparently found deep-seated pleasure in tormenting him about his 'untidy' life. 'Tim', Freya would begin in the evenings just when they had settled down a bottle of wine on the terrace, 'James and I have been thinking… time you settled down… head in sand… old enough now… thinking about the future… responsibility… have you thought…', and so on. Tim was now practised at blanking out pretty well everything she said and since the key phrases didn't change much, he got the drift of it without having to look at her or listen. Instead, he sniffed the scented air appreciatively and took another gulp at the ridiculously cheap but delicious wine they'd bought in the supermarket.

Freya was bad enough, but Tim was beginning to actively loathe her husband. What an insufferable prick he was dishing out 'fatherly' advice to him when he was only a couple of years older than he was. James was a headhunter whatever that was and earned a fortune doing fuck all, as far as Tim could tell, apart from suggesting friends of his from Harrow for high flyer jobs in the City and then coining in commission. James was now urging him to start as a teaboy or something in a firm like his and 'work his way up the ladder'. James was a master of cliché, Tim thought.

'I have a nobler calling, James', he now told him, yawning with the effort of keeping his eyes open after all the sun and wine.

'What, writing a novel that never gets finished, and doing scraps of work for magazines?' interrupted the beastly Freya. 'And living like a student in a rented flat with a leaking roof and no hot water when you're nearly 30?'

'My column on *GQ* is very highly regarded', retorted Tim indignantly, ignoring the unpalatable truth about the hovel in Battersea. 'Yes, 'Layabout around Town', said Freya. 'That just about sums you up. You really should grow up Tim.'

'Leave off Freya, since when have you done any work? You have a cleaner to clean your house, a nanny to look after your kids, and a fruit machine called James whose lever you pull every time you want cash.'

There had been several pointless conversations along these lines in the last week or two and Tim was glad to have escaped. Now strolling along in the sunshine from the formal Peyrou gardens, under the Arc de Triomphe built to glorify Louis XIV, and along the chic Rue Foch bordered by eighteenth century mansions housing smart shops at street level, a bold plan began to form in Tim's head.

He turned off Rue Foch and found himself in a maze of medieval alleyways, some of which opened out into unexpected squares with outdoor restaurants and chestnut trees. God this city was lovely. And the countryside around it was staggering too – the mountains, the wilderness of the surrounding countryside which the locals called the *garrigue*, the little villages, untouched really by the 20th century. And the things that mattered were so cheap – like wine and houses. Tim had looked in the estate agents' windows and was astonished by the low rents compared to England. Of course, he couldn't afford to buy anything here but anyone, he saw, who had a modest flat in London, could exchange it for whole house in Montpellier. Surely, he could afford to live here and finance himself by freelance journalism, and perhaps giving English lessons as well. And if that failed, he could work in a bar. His head swam with possibilities.

Glancing left up a small passageway, he noted with amusement a union jack and a couple of tables outside what looked like a bookshop. He climbed the steep stone steps that led to the entrance of Wuthering Heights and went in.

Gerald was heaving books around and staggered under the weight of one box as Tim came in. Tim bounded across – 'here, let me help.' Together they manoeuvred the crate of books down the steep, curving staircase. 'Thanks,' said Gerald gruffly. 'One of these days they'll find me at the bottom of these stairs crushed to death under one of these damn things. I think you're the first person who's seen me struggling and offered to help.'

Twenty minutes later, they were still talking. It was early afternoon and there weren't many people around. Tim had admired the shop, selected a few books he wanted and asked Gerald's advice about the region. He had also picked up Lance's book on the Languedoc. 'Is this any good?' he asked. Gerald looked rueful. 'Unfortunately, it is.'

'Why unfortunately?'

'Because the guy who wrote it is a total arsehole', said Gerald, 'but I have to admit that the book is an excellent introduction to the region if you're thinking of trying to settle here. He lives about forty minutes away in a village called Le Prairie near Vevey – now that area round there is a good place to set yourself up. There's quite a lot of English people there, some of them writers, and it's an extremely popular bit of the countryside, close to Montpellier and close to the sea. And Vevey's a splendid town. I can give you Lance's number if you like – rather you than me, but he has lived down there longer than most and he knows what the set up is down there. Just don't tell him I sent you'.

16

It wasn't until July that Jean Campion got a chance to see Judith on her own. Well, that wasn't strictly true. It wasn't until then that Jean plucked up courage to talk to Judith about what was bothering her so much. A victim of conflicting loyalties, like so many women who have long been married to bullying men and are accustomed to defending the indefensible, even to themselves, Jean hesitated before confronting her own fears. She didn't want to be disloyal to Lance and she was a little daunted by Judith. She seemed rather aloof – not unfriendly, but not very approachable either. Much more worrying, though, was what she might find out. When she thought about it, which she only permitted herself to do in the long watches of the night while Lance snorted and grunted beside her like a wounded buffalo, her stomach knotted and she sweated with apprehension.

Finally, on July 11th, she woke up and remembered it would have been Sarah's birthday – was Sarah's birthday. Is Sarah's birthday. Oh god, let her be alive and well. Happy would be good too, she thought. Happiness was an emotion Jean had felt slide away from herself years ago for good after Sarah went missing. She remembered someone telling her unhelpfully at the time that 'children are sent to punish us'. Well, she was being punished wasn't she? And perhaps she deserved punishing. That was one of the things she needed to know now. Could she have prevented this happening. Was there something she should have known, should have acted upon to make Sarah go. Had she turned a blind eye to something, the way she usually did? The 'something' in question was not anything that Jean was ready to put a name to or visualise. It was at the moment just a little, hard black stone of doubt.

At ten o'clock, Lance went off to play golf for the day with Frank Partridge Rex Stanhope and Alan Knight. They had a regular four and made a day of it. It was already in the 80s and creeping upwards. France was in the grip of a *canicule*, a heat wave that had started at the beginning of June and was to continue until September, killing off record numbers of old people. There had been no rain since May and Jean despaired of her garden. Everything was dying. The water that came out of her hosepipe was just a hot trickle and she didn't know what to aim it at first. The grass, such as it was, was already burnt stubble.

It was oppressive heat too, humid and cloying. It didn't suit Jean's fair skin at all and she felt dried up and enervated. It was an effort to move or go anywhere. Getting in the car was torture in itself. The metal of the door was as hot to the touch as an iron, the seat burned and everything smelled of melting rubber and plastic. Curiously, Lance seemed to thrive on this weather. It made him more excitable, more lion-like than ever. Also, more belligerent, at least towards her. She hoped he would take out his aggression on the golf ball today… how he could even think of playing golf on a day like this, she didn't know. But, good riddance. She had time to herself; it was a day for action then. She knew she would call Judith.

Judith was comatose on her roof terrace when the call came from Jean. She had only meant to come up for a short time to read yesterday's paper and feel the sun on her face before an afternoon's tutorials, but had dozed off on a lounger after attempting to revive her dying geraniums. Jean's call caught her unawares. Without explanation, Jean, whom she hardly knew, had asked if she could drop by before lunch. Sleepily, Judith agreed. It was only when she put the phone down that she began to worry. What could Jean want? Was this a friendly, inconsequential call, or not. She hadn't really ever thought about Jean except to pity her for being married to Lance. Jenny Knight had once mentioned in passing what a doormat she was when it came to Lance which, she thought, was why Lance got away with his arrogance. But she, Judith, had formed no opinion of her at all. She had been too busy hating her husband. She hoped that whatever it was wouldn't take long.

Thus, she was completely unprepared for what came next. When Jean arrived, Judith offered her a coffee but Jean only asked for water. She sat at the kitchen table taking small sips and nervously pushing back damp strands of her grey-blonde hair which fell out of the knot at the back of her head whilst gulping for air like a stranded goldfish.

'What is it, Jean?' Judith asked gently. She could see the woman was very anxious and now her eyes suddenly swam with tears. 'Judith, I don't know how to put this,' said Jean, haltingly, 'but I have to ask you something. I hope you don't mind and I don't like doing this but please, I need you to tell me the truth. It may be nothing, but it may be something…' She broke off. 'It's about Lance', she blurted then, 'I know you saw him a couple of months back in Vevey – you said so at the Knights' barbeque, do you remember, and Lance was cross….'

Judith nodded, now feeling fearful herself. 'What was he doing, Judith?'

'Are you sure you need to know?'

'I'm sure. Please.'

'He was… embracing somebody', said Judith finally. Her voice had come out like a squeak. 'It may not have meant anything, Jean'.

'Was it Sophie Stanhope?' asked Jean, her head in her hands now.

'Yes'. Judith was relieved she didn't have to say the name. Jean must have suspected.

'Was that what you told Lance… that you'd seen him with Sophie?' Jean asked.

'Yes. He didn't like it,' Judith said now. 'That was when he called you over.'

'Did you say anything to Rex and Camilla?'

'I thought about it but I knew it was none of my business. I wanted to because I thought it was wrong. Sophie's only fourteen or fifteen, but she seems older I know. I'm so sorry, Jean. This must be difficult for you'.

'It's so much more difficult than you think'. Jean now openly wept. 'It's not that I care what Lance does. This isn't about me and him. It's about what's happened in the past. This just confirms it. I can't talk about it though Judith. I just can't; at least not now. Thank you for telling me. Please can I just ask you not to mention this to anybody for the time being? I have to go away and think about what I must do.' She got up and for a moment Judith hugged her before she let herself out.

'Do what you have to do Jean,' she said. 'I won't say anything if you don't want me to, but please, come and talk to me again if you want to. I don't like to see you like this. And… and, take care', she added lamely as Jean left. Suddenly, she felt frightened for her as well as desperately sad.

Tim decided to take Gerald's advice to go and see Lance Campion and look around Vevey. He had telephoned Lance in advance who had suggested they meet at Café Le Square. He was rather looking forward to it. Gerald's description of Lance as an arsehole amused him. Certainly the fruity voice on the phone and the fact that Lance had suggested he could possibly 'squeeze' him in to his hectic schedule later on in the week in order to give him a 'few pointers' about the region had hinted at pomposity. Lance evidently regarded himself in relation to the Languedoc as Peter Mayle was to Provence. 'Lance of the Languedoc v. Peter of Provence' thought Tim delightedly. He could feel a feature coming on. All at once he felt certain that he should take the risk and move down here for a while. There must be loads of freelance features he could write for the papers back home given the current obsession of the English with this part of the world.

As he drove in the shimmering heat through the countryside down towards Vevey his spirits lifted. The wide open spaces of the *garrigue* with the blue mountains in the distance were breathtaking. There was just so much space and air. The tiny medieval villages he passed were so untouched by time too and seemingly deserted. Any village that pretty in England would be overrun by rubberneckers in July he thought, cramming into chintzy pubs by rivers to eat filthy fast food in 'olde worlde' style. A bolt of hatred for his native land shot through him. He hoped he wouldn't find too many Brits down near Vevey but there again, there was enough space for them all to get lost in down here. And, he supposed, they would at least be the discerning ones who, like himself, appreciated the quality of life here. Yes, he thought, things are definitely looking up.

His euphoria dissipated somewhat as an hour later he sat trapped in Café Le Square with a terracotta-faced Lance who was droning on at great length about himself over a second *pichet* of red wine. He had heard all about 'My life as an advertising whizz kid tycoon' and now Lance was on to 'My life as a celebrated author in France'. Tim knew that his role as Lance's new audience was to look fascinated and in awe of this model of older manhood – god the man fancied himself – but he supposed that eventually Lance would pause for breath and then he might find out something useful.

Finally satisfied that he had sufficiently impressed his young guest, Lance leaned back happily and looked at Tim. 'So, what brings you down to this part of the world?' he asked. Tim explained that he was a freelance journalist and that he wanted to sound out Lance about the possibility of making a living in the area from his writing, perhaps supplemented by teaching English or working in some other field. He also needed to find somewhere to rent. Lance, who rather liked the look of Tim and thought he might be an agreeable addition to the community – at least he was reasonably intelligent and seemed to appreciate Lance's stories – always a good sign – decided to be helpful.

'As it happens, I've got just the place for you to rent if you decide to stay,' he said. 'I own a couple of *gîtes* just up the road, one of which has just become vacant. It's small but comfortable – one bedroom – and has a small terrace at the back. I wouldn't charge you much long-term. And as for work, you'll find you don't need to earn as much as you do in the UK. I should think you could easily keep yourself for a while especially if you get a regular freelance slot on some publication rabbiting on about life in the Midi – you know the sort of thing – 'Letters from the Languedoc' – or something. They lap it up back home. I'm always being approached by various Sunday supplements for that kind of stuff and I have to turn it down – I could push some of it your way, if you like.'

'That would be splendid,' said Tim. 'I appreciate it. And I'd love to look at the *gîte*.'

A deal was struck that afternoon and greatly elated, Tim returned to Montpellier with a new sense of purpose. He would go back to England, pack up there, sub-let his flat and come back to La Prairie within a week or two. Lance had come up trumps after all. The *gîte* was fine, he loved the area and he now felt confident enough to make a go of things down here. In addition, he'd had a brainwave which he'd mentioned to Lance. What about starting a local newsletter – a sort of local newspaper for the ex-pat community that he could write and print on his computer. He could charge enough to cover his expenses and it would be a good way to get to know everybody as well as to garner material for freelance features and columns in the UK. Humming a little tune as he drove back at speed a little worse for wear but in excellent spirits, he thought happily about telling the insufferable Freya and James about his future plans. 'Get a life', they'd told him. Well, he just did. And it was going to be a damn sight better than theirs.

17

That July was intensely hot even for the south of France. There had been no rain since May and even the village housewives, accustomed to heat, would fan themselves in the street or the shops. '*Oooh, il fait chaud!*' they said to each other in passing. Everything and everybody was visibly wilting and by 11 am most people were off the streets; even the colony of dogs who seemed to belong to nobody and trotted around purposefully most of the time as if on important missions, skulked in the shadows or perhaps took themselves off to the cemetery where at least they could lie in the shade of the columns of cypress trees which stood guard over the ornate tombstones topped by grave-faced angels.

Opposite Judith, the family of Spanish extraction who seemed to live on picnic chairs outside their front door from teatime onwards, often joined by members of their extended family, now only ventured out after dusk. The wife, a small, busy creature in an overall nevertheless seemed to be the only person who wasn't slowed down by the heavy heat. Speaking voluble Spanish all the time, she vigorously swept her stoop several times a day until every tile was gleaming. Then at dusk she would come out with a bucket of water which she proceeded to sprinkle alongside the row of chairs where her friends and family were gathered. This puzzled Judith. Was it to settle the dust, or what? Nobody took any notice at all, so it perhaps was an established custom. Then one night, she and her silent husband started skinning a hare outside, she holding it up by its legs as he ripped its fur off with a knife until its entrails were visible and its blood gushed into the gutter where it ran down the length of the street. The stench of the blood, exacerbated by the dry, still air, lingered for hours making Judith nauseous. Peasant life was all very well, she thought, but she'd rather not have to witness it.

These long humid nights, Judith found she could only sleep if she decamped to the basement bedroom where the sun couldn't penetrate through the small ventilation grill that passed for a window at street level and the room stayed relatively cool. Even so, she reckoned she heard the church clock chime most of the hours and she awoke in the morning damp and unrefreshed. In the daytime most of the house above street level was too hot for comfort. Neither opening all the windows, nor closing them, seemed to help. Oh for air conditioning: but that was commonplace only in the very pink and elaborate new villas built on the outskirts of Vevey for the Northern French exiles who favoured second homes in the region.

As for the roof terrace, it had become unbearable, even in the shade of the large vine that hung over one corner and was home to many oversized angry wasps, and stayed that way until well past dark. The tiles underfoot were too hot to walk on and all her potted plants had literally burnt to death. You're supposed to like the heat, she told the geraniums crossly but they were past hearing her.

In the mornings her kitchen, dominated by an old pine table brought over from England, was too hot to linger in, and since this room doubled as her study, she had to change her habits and work in the afternoons when the sun had swung over to the other side of the house and she could sit at the table writing poetry or preparing lessons for her growing band of pupils. grateful for the tiny breeze generated by the creaking electric fan overhead.

In the week after she had talked to Gerald at Wuthering Heights, she had felt inspired to write more poetry. She hadn't had the energy or inclination to do this for some months but Gerald's remarks about Howard Hill had encouraged her, even though he couldn't know this. She had thought quite a bit about Gerald lately. He was so completely different from most of the people she had met down here who were so in your face. Horrid expression but descriptive. There was a kind of terrible neediness about some of the British down here. They had made the move to a foreign country but they were still looking for reassurance that they had done the right thing. Clearly the French weren't going to embrace them like brothers so they needed you to make up a part of their tight-knit community, and being British, they wanted to place you too.

Were you a Surrey stockbroker? No? A Bolton barmaid then? Not that either. When Judith had explained that she was a teacher who had tired of teaching in England, they understood that. What they felt uneasy about was her status. Why was she still single? Was she a divorcee? Did she have a lover, did she want a lover, what was she after? They didn't of course dare to phrase those questions in that way but Judith could tell that they were desperate to know the answers. She was too unknowable for them and they didn't like that. The more they tried to cosy up to her, the more she retreated. She hadn't even been to the Saturday barbeque for a couple of weeks. Either they thought that she was a crashing snob or a mysterious recluse; she thought she knew which.

Gerald however had not asked any personal questions at all, not even where she was living, and she knew that he was the kind of man who would wait for you to volunteer information rather than drag it out of you. Their talk had been strictly confined to literature and yet, even so, Judith felt that he was a man she could trust. She had seen something on television about the way the human brain immediately made evaluations of new people's faces forming instant judgements about every aspect of personality but especially whether they were trustworthy – because, she supposed, it was necessary to survival. If you were a more primitive animal, you would run, if you saw someone or something you couldn't trust. Nowadays, you had to endure sitting next to them at dinner parties for hours on end if you were unlucky. Inevitably, Lance came to mind, with his too pale eyes and his cruel mouth. And yet others presumably did trust him or had trusted him.

Look at poor Jean – she must have trusted him once. She hadn't seen Jean since she had come to see her and doubted whether she would get in touch again. It had obviously been an ordeal for her to come and talk to her that day and what she learned must have been mortifying. She would probably be embarrassed to see Judith just now. She wondered what Jean had meant when she had said it mattered because of something that had happened in the past. She supposed she was referring to previous affairs that Lance had had, or perhaps suspected he had.

He was not the sort of man who would ever have been faithful for long; he would always have craved the adulation of new people. Poor Jean, she thought again, but what could she really do to help? She could never go round to see her in case Lance was there but anyway she hardly knew the woman; she just hoped she had somebody else to support her. Sooner or later she was bound to bump into her but naturally she wouldn't say anything unless Jean brought it up first.

In fact it was a while before she saw Jean again. But by that time she was in reluctant possession of some new explosive information about Lance and everything had changed, were that possible, for the worse.

18

Rose was in Vevey looking for something decent to wear to impress her friend Milly who was due to arrive the next day for a week. It was the summer holidays and her parents once again had her dragged over to their French holiday house for the best part of the summer. This time, however, Rose wasn't so sulky about it as she had arranged for various friends to come over and stay and she looked forward to showing off her smattering of French and local knowledge. It also meant that she could hang around cafes and even bars in the evening if she was with a friend. This in turn meant meeting other people her age – perhaps some fit French boys, you never knew. In addition she was liberated from the exam pressure which she'd felt in May. She had sat her GCSE exams for better or worse the previous month and they hadn't been as bad as she feared. In any case there was nothing she could do about them now except await the results in late August.

All in all, the future looked bright – or brighter than usual anyway. Plus, today she felt flush, armed as she was with fifty Euros to spend on anything she liked – birthday money given to her for her sixteenth at the beginning of

July. Trouble was, the shops were pretty crap in Vevey. Where was Gap, where was New Look, where was River Island? Rose despaired. How could French teenagers manage? Looking at a crowd of them now laughing and pushing each other off the pavement as they walked along the main street in their lunch break, she could see that they didn't. They were still wearing things that went out years ago in Britain – well, last year anyhow. Poor them. What was irritating, though, was how thin all the girls were. She supposed it was because they weren't fed the diet of stodge she got at school. I bet they only eat salad all day she thought furiously. Some of the boys were quite cute though; she wondered whether they could speak English. It might be hard-going in the bars if they couldn't communicate at all.

As she turned the corner into the historic quarter she spotted Judith sitting having coffee on her own with her nose in a newspaper. She hadn't given her a thought since the coaching session at half term, but now she realised she was pleased to see her and walked over to say hello.

'Rose', exclaimed Judith. 'Are you back for the summer?'

'Yes, but I don't mind so much because I've got friends coming out for some parts of it and I'm also going to stay with some people in Provence at the end of this month.'

Judith told her to sit down and ordered her a coffee. 'Have you seen anything of Sophie?' she asked. 'I haven't seen her around these holidays.'

Rose suddenly remembered the conversation they had

had about Lance and Judith telling her to warn Sophie not to go out to dinner with him. She bit her lip, unsure whether to tell Judith what she knew.

After half term when they were both back at school, Rose had been surprised and rather pleased to get a text message from Sophie saying that she had to talk to her and could they meet as soon as the exams were over? She would ask her parents to invite Rose to stay for a couple of days at the first opportunity. Rose was intrigued by the invitation and texted back that she'd love to come before going out to France.

Once she had arrived in Oxfordshire and the girls were safely in Sophie's part of the house – she didn't just have a bedroom, but a whole floor to herself now that the boys had left home – Sophie disconcertingly burst in tears and sat on the floor sobbing whilst Rose hunted for tissues, both alarmed for her, and not a little excited at this unexpected development. At last Sophie calmed down enough to blurt out what had happened the night Lance took her out to dinner. Rose had forgotten about the dinner because she had gone back to England with her parents the following day. Now she listened with mounting horror as Sophie told her story between bouts of crying.

Apparently, everything was fine until Lance had ordered more and more wine at dinner and Sophie thought she was going to faint. The room started spinning and Lance had suggested a walk along the beach to clear her head.

Once on the beach which was completely dark, they walked for about ten minutes before Lance guided her to a sheltered spot in among some sand dunes. 'Then he completely changed', sniffed Sophie. 'Up until then with me he'd been sweet and just nicely flirtatious. Yes, he had tried to kiss me once before in Vevey but it was quite gentle and romantic and I thought that was all he'd try. After all, he's an old man! I thought he couldn't think I would want to go any further with him. I know I encouraged him, but I sort of thought it was safe considering he knows my parents and everybody. I thought he just wanted to show off being with a young girl around town and I wanted everyone to think how grown up I was. Oh god, I was so stupid! It was like he suddenly turned into a nasty, snarling animal on that beach. He fell on top of me, literally, and started tearing my clothes off whilst pulling my head back with my hair. I was terrified and trying to tell him to stop but he wouldn't and my face was all squashed by him so I could hardly breathe let alone scream. My t-shirt was all torn and then he yanked down my jeans whilst still holding me down. You can guess what happened next. In fact I'm not sure it did happen. I was so hysterical and hurting all over that I can't really tell. And the things he was saying, Rose, the horrible words he said all the time when this was going on'… a fresh bout of sobbing. 'What words?' breathed Rose. By now she was holding Sophie, pushing her damp hair out of her eyes and crying a little herself because it was so horrible.

'Words like 'whore' and 'bitch' and the c-word all the time, and things like he would kill me if I screamed and how I wanted it and stuff like that. It was like a nightmare. I kept thinking of my parents and what they would say and how it would be when they found me dead. I… I thought he was going to kill me, Rose.'

'How did it end? How did you stop him?'

'We heard noises nearby. I think there was a caravan site behind the dunes and there were some people walking nearby. Lance got off me and dragged me up with him. He sort of frogmarched me along the beach telling me to pull myself together and not to make a sound. When we got to his car he pushed me inside and drove off fast. I was past fighting by this time. Everything hurt, especially my head and I kept almost losing consciousness. I couldn't even cry. It was like being in a bad dream. The next thing we were back at my house which was empty because my parents were away.

Lance pretended to be nice again then and told me he was sorry if he had hurt me, but that I had wanted to make love by moonlight – that's what he said 'make love by moonlight', and that he wanted to make me happy. He said he didn't mean to be so rough but that some girls liked that. He got me into the shower to clean up and then he put me in bed. He kept telling me that I mustn't tell anybody what happened because nobody would believe me. He said everyone knew that I was a little fantasist and that everybody had seen me flirting with him.

After that I must have fallen asleep and he must have gone home. When I woke up it was light and he wasn't there. I lay there for ages quite still in case he was but I was hurting so much and aching everywhere that I finally got up to find some painkillers. When I looked at my body in the mirror I couldn't stop crying; there were bruises and cuts everywhere. But then I realised that my parents would be back that day and I already knew that I couldn't tell them about it, so I just wore baggy clothes and even though my face was all swollen and puffy, they didn't even really notice. I just said I had a bad headache and felt sick probably because of having a bad mussel or something the night before. Anyway, everyone was in a rush because we had to fly back that night and the next day I went back to school.

'Oh, Sophie,' said Rose, 'How did you cope at school? Did you tell anyone?'

'I couldn't tell anyone. I was so ashamed of myself and anyway I believed Lance when he said that no-one would believe me. He was right. I've often boasted about things that didn't really happen at school so it would be like crying wolf or whatever. And if they had believed me, they would have called me a dirty slag and I would have got a terrible reputation. I couldn't win either way. I just tried to blank it out and concentrate on work which I did. Only I kept having these crying jags when I didn't expect it – like my body was still unhappy even if I wasn't if you know what I mean. You were the only person I wanted to tell, Rose. Partly because you know Lance, and partly because I thought you would understand. You're a kind person I can tell. I don't know anyone else like you at my school and I had to talk to someone.'

Rose hugged her tightly. 'Of course you did,' she said. 'And I do understand and I'm so, so sorry for you. But shouldn't you tell someone, your parents or the police? Because you've been raped, Sophie, and you can't keep this to yourself.'

But, Rose thought now, as she sat with Judith two weeks later in the sun, Sophie was absolutely clear that she didn't want anyone else to know. In fact after that terrible outburst, Sophie had seemed OK for the rest of her stay. Clearly, she was not the same Sophie Stanhope as the one of two months previously who had lorded it over Rose and acted like she was twenty-five; but she was a lot nicer. Some of the stuffing had been knocked out of her and if she had lost confidence and had a nasty shock then she had also lost her conceit and precocity. Rose liked the new Sophie a lot, and felt nothing but pity for her. All that showing off before had just been an act. When, as Rose was leaving, Sophie thanked her for being such a good friend to her, Rose got the impression that all Sophie had ever wanted for someone to pay her a little attention. It made her sad.

Now, with Judith, she was very torn. She had kept Sophie's secret but she was still very concerned for her and outraged by Lance's behaviour. The man should be arrested. Judith, she felt, was possibly the one sensible adult she could trust with the secret. She knew everybody involved but was distanced from them; she was also understanding and Rose felt she would be sympathetic without becoming hysterical. Rose realised that for the past couple of weeks she had been carrying a dreadful burden on Sophie's behalf and now that the opportunity presented itself, she very much wanted to offload it. Judith, she sensed, would know what to do. She began to tell her the story.

19

Just across the street from where Rose and Judith were having coffee, Fern was dusting the dangling coloured glass lanterns in the shop where she had found work in Vevey. It was kind of shop Fern adored, full of what her mother would have called knick-knacks. In other words, the kind of things one had no need for whatsoever but appealed to tourists who felt the urge to spend money. Although the shop had a French name, L'Étoile Clair, it had a definite Eastern hippy feel to it. The sweet cloying scent of incense was always in the air and there was a brisk trade in associated artefacts such as candles, joss sticks, hookah pipes and herbal soaps. The clothes they had were floaty cheesecloth numbers, some of them with elaborate beading which came direct from India where they were no doubt run up in sweat shops by children. Fern didn't like to think about this, but otherwise she approved of the merchandise. It had exactly the kind of things she herself liked to linger over like essential oils, silver earrings and small, carved cedar-wood boxes. She knew that back in England these kind of shops were completely outdated and had been replaced by more sophisticated chains like Monsoon, but she was perfectly happy floating around in this sixties time-warp shop in her own black cheesecloth shift caught up at the waist in a butterfly belt.

With her blonde bob and face burnished by the sun, she looked well and pretty and a million times better than she had back in Bicester, her white face pinched by cold and unhappiness. Sure, she had been lonely at first, but now she had a rented flat she could afford, a comfortable job and was beginning to make friends. Miriam, the French girl who owned the shop was a bit younger than her but she spoke good English and had been very kind to her, introducing her to regular customers and other shop owners nearby so that Fern now knew a number of both French and English people with whom she could have a drink or pass the time of day. Her only worry – and it was a big one – was Ben.

He had been so amenable about coming to France and leaving behind his beloved football and close circle of friends. Like her, he had thought it a bit of an adventure and was prepared to give it his best. He hadn't even made a fuss about going to the local school half way through a term and being plunged into an entirely foreign system with little grasp of the language. She had been so proud of him, especially since at first he was evidently a kind of star attraction and he had boasted to her about all the new slang he was picking up and the friends he was beginning to make.

This initial buoyancy hadn't lasted very long however and now Ben would hardly talk about school, beyond saying that the work was very hard. When Fern tried to ask him about his friends there and whether he would like to bring any of them home, he clammed up. French kids, according to him, didn't go to each others' houses; they all had to be home for the family meal at 6pm and then they had to do homework. None of them seemed to do any sport after school, or if they did, they were driven to private clubs which Ben didn't know about. He became quiet and withdrawn and went up to his room as soon as he returned from school, refusing to discuss his day with her.

Becoming increasingly anxious about him, Fern finally plucked up courage to go to speak to the *Directrice* of his school. It was a difficult interview. Madame Jospert was a formidable middle-aged lady with scarlet finger nails and a bun, the kind of tough efficient French woman to be found in all corners of the great lumbering bureaucracy which penetrated every area of French life, dedicated to doing things by the book. School was evidently just an adjunct to her of the civil service and she clearly had little patience with Fern's stammered anxieties about her son's welfare.

'*C'est normal*', was her considered shrugged response to Fern's worries about Ben's lack of friends, difficulties with the work and the language and apparent unhappiness. The subtext, Fern thought grimly, was what did she expect – an incompetent Englishwoman turning up in the middle of the school year with a teenage son who had no chance of passing the baccalaureate and little hope of fitting in. She had cried afterwards and determined to take Ben away and if necessary find him another school or scrape up enough money for private coaching. Her heart quailed at the thought of having to return home, but she knew she would do it if it was what Ben needed to do.

But Ben had been adamant that this was not what he wanted. 'Don't worry, mum, it'll be OK,' he told her that night. 'I can hack it. And in any case, I couldn't go back to Bicester now. All my friends have done their exams there now and some of them have even left school. I wouldn't fit in there now either.'

Things seemed to get a little better after Fern met Judith in the shop and got talking to her about Ben. Judith had suggested that if Ben's French improved, then it might be easier for him to integrate and had offered to coach him once or twice a week. Fern accepted gladly and was grateful that Judith (sensing Fern's desperation and lack of money) had offered to do it for next to nothing. 'It'll be good for me to keep my hand in at teaching', she said after she'd met Ben, whom she liked and felt sorry for. He was clearly lonely but trying hard to cope. After that, Ben seemed to cheer up a bit and his French had certainly improved.

Now Fern was more relaxed about Ben. All of a sudden he seemed almost like his old self again, almost light-hearted. He was a funny boy though. Just lately, he had become fanatical about sorting out his room which had formerly been reassuringly squalid. He had got several black bin liners and had thrown out a huge amount of junk. Also, she knew for a fact that he was planning to give away several of his favourite things such as books and CDs. He had asked Fern for some wrapping paper and said he was going to give them to all his friends back home as Christmas presents even though it was only July. When she mentioned this to Judith, she had looked thoughtful. 'That's odd', she said, 'I meant to mention to you that Ben gave me something too recently – a rather beautiful statue of a tiger carved from soapstone. Of course I said I couldn't accept it, but he insisted.'

'But he loves that statue,' cried Fern. 'It was one of the few things his father gave him… I can't believe he gave you that. I'm glad he gave you a present of course – you've been such a help to him, but I'm very surprised it was that.' Fern determined to speak to Ben that evening. What on earth was he doing giving all these things away. And she was a bit unnerved about his room now. She'd been pleased at first because it had been such a mess but his behaviour was a bit strange – she wondered with a sudden pang of anxiety whether he was planning to run away or something. That evening at home she poured herself a drink and waited anxiously for Ben to come back. She must talk to him. But when he did return, he was evasive as usual.

'I don't have to justify giving presents to people I like', he told Fern. 'I'm bored of all my clutter, that's all.'

He went upstairs and she could hear the door slam. I suppose he's on his bloody computer, she thought. I wish I'd never saved up to buy him that – it seems to have taken him over. Just lately, Ben had spent every evening on it, only coming down, reluctantly to eat supper. Once, a couple of nights back she had got up in the night and seen his light still on at 2am and heard him still tapping away. When she remonstrated with him, he told her he had an essay to finish that he'd forgotten about.

Early the morning after she and Judith had talked about Ben in the shop, Judith rang her. 'Is Ben still there?' she asked.

'No, you've just missed him. He's gone to school.'

'Fern, can I come round?' Judith sounded anxious.

Fern told her she could come round straight away before she had to go and open the shop. Suddenly she felt rather afraid. This was an odd request from Judith.

'Why? What's up? Is it about Ben?'

But Judith didn't say. 'I'll be with you in fifteen minutes,' she said and put the phone down.

20

Today was the day. Ben stood at his window looking down in the street below. He tried to focus on the plane tree opposite but the more he tried, the more it became blurred, its leaves fusing into a great green blob. It was just before dawn and he hadn't slept all night because his head was buzzing – not with excitement exactly but with something indefinable, a feeling of great lightness and emptiness. It was a high of sorts though not like any high he had ever achieved through smoking weed. He felt unanchored, unrooted like a spec of dust dancing in the air. A title of a book he'd noticed in a bookshop came to him: *The Unbearable Lightness of Being.* That was it, that was exactly how he was feeling now. The odd thing was that with this strange buzzy lightness, came no feeling whatsoever. He knew he should feel something on this day of days but he just couldn't. He tried now to summon a feeling purely as an experiment, but it wouldn't come, not even when he thought of his mother. Normally, thinking of Fern with her pretty, anxious face and evident concern for him simultaneously gave his heart a tug and made him feel guilty, but not now. It was as if his neural connections had all been pulled out of their sockets – how weird was that? And how good was that too? Feelings were bad, and feelings had to be stopped. And somehow, in the last few weeks, he had achieved that by thinking only of his plan, his solution – and it had worked. If he had any feelings, he would probably take the time to tell all the unhappy people in the universe how he had achieved this, because surely everyone would like to know how to stop their own feelings. The only people who completely understood him were the people he had found in the suicide chatroom, Chatting to Death.

These people who came from all over the world had become his closest friends because they all had the same interest in common – ending their lives. It was all they talked about but it was never boring because in discussing their deaths and all the detailed planning that was going into it, they also discussed their lives. There were some who had been at it for years apparently, which when Ben started corresponding, he had found ironic. Often though, he learned, they had tried and been 'rescued' by well-meaning friends and relatives. What was strange was how it was sometimes the other chatroom correspondents who had called the police or whatever; on the other hand, some of them positively encouraged action. 'Go on then, do it. Keep going' read one message when one of their number whose sign-on was Eyeball told them all how many prescription drugs he had just taken. Ben never did learn whether Eyeball lived or not but he had stopped corresponding so perhaps he had managed it.

He himself had particularly struck up a relationship with a girl in California whose sign-on was Penfox. Penfox was cool. She was a little older than him but she looked out for him. Every day she wrote: 'How are you today?' like she really cared. And when he replied that he couldn't take it anymore, she urged him to reconsider. She told him that she had been suicidal for as long as she could remember and yet there was no reason for it that she could think of. Her family was cool and her school had been OK; she just never felt comfortable inside her life. She said she kept hanging on though hoping it would change one day whilst knowing it wouldn't. The chatroom was her only way of getting any relief from her ongoing depression.

It was like that with most of them – they knew these guys, their virtual friends really, really understood what they were going through, unlike all the doctors and psychiatrists they were sent to see. Ben had been careful not to correspond with Penfox in the last 24 hours in case she realised how near he was getting to his time and tried to trace him or something. He didn't want anything getting in his way now.

When Judith arrived at Fern's, she wasted no time. 'There may be nothing to worry about, Fern, but on the other hand there just may be,' she said quickly. 'Don't ask questions now but just telephone Ben's school and check whether he got there. Could I go up to his room and look at his computer?'

Fern felt icy cold and faint. She didn't want to face up to what Judith's concern suggested. Deliberately, she pushed down her feeling of rising panic. 'He won't have got there yet anyway,' she said angrily. 'Judith, what is this? Why don't you think Ben will be there? Has he said something to you?' But Judith was half way up the stairs. 'Phone as soon as he should be there', she called. 'I won't be long. I just need to check something'.

Heart hammering now, hoping against hope that she was wrong, she booted up Ben's computer and looked around her at his transformed room, almost empty of possessions, de-personalised. No note. Bed made, unslept in probably. Everything uncannily neat. A life put on hold, or tidied away. Quickly she scanned the computer screen and accessed the internet with no difficulty, Ben's password being automatic. In the space you typed the website address you wanted, she clicked on the arrow to the side to scroll down the recent sites he had accessed.

There was only one, dozens and dozens of time over. Sweating now, she double-clicked on it. Please let me be wrong, she intoned to herself, please, please… She didn't need to read much. It was what she feared and now she needed to act fast. 'Fern', she shouted, but Fern was already half way up the stairs. 'He's not at school, she whispered, her voice breaking, the panic rising again like the gorge in her throat. 'He hasn't shown up this morning. Where is he? What are you doing? What's this all about?' She started to cry. 'What do you know about this, Judith? Where is Ben?'

Judith tried to get a grip on herself. Fern mustn't become hysterical because they had to think hard and act fast, but she had to let her know her fears for Ben. 'I'm worried that Ben might be thinking of harming himself,' she told Fern. 'He's been looking up a suicide site on the internet where people talk about suicide and ways of doing it. And he's cleared out his room and given things away – it can be a sign, you see Fern, that he's thinking of giving up. But I might be wrong. Please don't cry yet.'

Fern was now hugging herself, swaying slightly, shoulders heaving silently, tears streaming down her cheeks – 'Please Fern, the most important thing we can do now for Ben is to find him before anything happens. He may just have gone somewhere to think, to get away from school.' She held Fern in her arms. 'Think now, Fern, think where he might have gone. Does he have a favourite place to go? He can't have gone far. We can go and look for him now.'

'He has a bike', Fern gulped. 'He goes off into the country sometimes on it at weekends. He says he likes to walk in the *garrigue* and if it's hot he goes swimming. He doesn't take it to school cos he walks there. She ran down the stairs. 'It's gone!' she wailed. 'Oh god, where is he. Where can he be?'

'Think, Fern, think,' urged Judith. 'Where might he go to be alone? Be strong now and think. We need to find him. Who else might know? Get in my car now and we'll drive to all the places within cycling distance that he might go. He's been gone less than an hour; he can't have gone too far. Where would he swim round here? In the river? The only river beach I know is too far away. Is there anywhere else?

21

Lance of the Languedoc, as Tim had privately dubbed him, was feeling pretty chipper. He and Alan Knight had thrashed Frank Partridge and Rex Stanhope on the golf course once again, even though it was really a damned sight too hot to play. Now, he thought, there was just time to shower and change and then he could bowl along to Roland's for a drink and chat before he closed up for the afternoon. Roland had mentioned that he had some pretty special white burgundy put away behind the bar and also they needed to finalise their plans for a trip to a particular club in Montpellier.

He was less than pleased to encounter the buffoon Bill Bailey half an hour later on his way out of Café Le Square. Bill's angry, red sweating face could not just be put down to the heat. 'Those bloody buggers don't deserve your custom if that's where you're heading,' he shouted across the street to Lance gesticulating in the direction of Roland's. Lance sighed and stopped reluctantly by Bill's jammy open-top silver Mercedes.

'What seems to be the problem?' he asked, fanning himself with his panama.

'Not *seems* to be the problem – *is* the bloody problem', said Bill furiously. 'Not content with refusing to sell me the damn place at a far higher price than those monkeys deserve, they are now refusing to serve me a beer. I wouldn't have gone there except it's the only goddamned bar for miles around and I needed a cigar.

'A cigar?' queried Lance, interested. 'They haven't started selling Havanas have they?' He too would be up for one of those.

'No, of course not, that would be way beyond their limited Gallic imaginations. They sell some kind of French variety, naturally, filled with something like crushed-up deckchairs, but it's better than nothing and I haven't got time to go into Montpellier to get any Cohibas. Anyway, I mentioned that they could do with getting in some decent cigars and they virtually threw me out. That appalling little peasant you hang out with, Roland, started ranting on about Jose Bove, whoever he might be, and telling me to go back where I belong.'

Lance felt his temper rising. He too would like Bill Bailey to go back where he came from. It was difficult enough getting on with the natives without blundering idiots like Bill alienating them altogether. He, like Judith, had noticed a few anti-English and American slogans daubed on walls in the area lately and was a little alarmed. As for Roland invoking José Bove – that was seriously bad news. Bove was the French peasant leader who in 1999 trashed a McDonald's under construction near Montpellier, instantly becoming a national resistance hero, his influence being particular strong in La France Profonde where it was hard to find a motorway bridge without it calling for Bove's release from jail, where in fact he had only languished for six weeks after Lionel Jospin called his action 'just'. Which in a way it was, since the Americans had unilaterally imposed trade restrictions on the superb local Roquefort cheese. If there was going to be no Roquefort in the US, Bove's argument went, then why should the French tolerate the 'McMerde' burger in France which in any case was bad for French farmers who produced the proper stuff.

Briefly, he explained to Bill who Bove was, adding, 'So look here, Bill, we definitely do not want another peasants' revolt down here. Unfortunately, the locals tend to confuse us with the Americans and we can't afford to fall out with them. You have to try to be more diplomatic.'

Bill's face turned a darker shade of magenta were that possible. 'Diplomatic?' he spluttered. 'What they need is an automatic – aimed at their temples. There's no reasoning with them. Buggers all caved into the Germans at the start of the war and have been blaming us for it ever since. Can't take the guilt. We'll never get on with them, and you're kidding yourself if you think you can with your fancy manners and panama hat. I tell you, if it weren't for my business interests here, I'd leave tomorrow.' So saying, he slammed his car door and fired the engine.

'Well, maybe that would be best', countered Lance but his words were lost in the roar of the Mercedes' turbo engine and his panama flew off in the slipstream of fuel and dust that Bill left in his wake. 'Fucking fool,' he said angrily out loud, stooping to retrieve his hat from the gutter. He strode towards the bar in time to see to Roland pulling down the shutters and locking up. Frantically he gesticulated to him to open up but Roland ignored him. What was he playing at? Don't say that all the Brits were barred now on account of that jumped-up cretin. He sighed deeply, wiping the sweat from his brow and noting the beginnings of a tension headache. There was nothing for it but to head off home to Jean's unwelcoming face – what had got into her lately? – and a limp salad if he was lucky. Not exactly a bower of bliss there either.

A few miles away Tim was contentedly lying on his back on the grass at the edge of a dam which the locals used to swim in at the weekends. Dressed only in his shorts and with yesterday's *Tribune* covering his eyes from the glare of the sun, he was thinking how fortunate it was that events had propelled him down here, starting, he supposed with that ridiculous school feature. He wondered what had happened to that Carinthia who had spun him the story? She had been a piece of work! Life in the south of France was suiting him down to the ground. He adored the heat and the countryside, was very comfortable in his bachelor *gîte*, had fixed up a surprising amount of freelance journalistic work already – but not so much that he couldn't afford not to be at desk – and was looking forward to getting to know some of the local talent. The girls were ten times better looking than their London counterparts. Thin and sexy and stylish in a way that had nothing to do with the clothes they wore – rather the way they wore them.

Luckily, his French wasn't bad. Being musical, he had a good ear for it and he was sure he could pick it up in no time… here, his reverie was interrupted by his dog pushing his newspaper off his nose and licking his face with meaty breath. 'Get off, Piggy'. He sat up and threw a stick for her into the water which she bounded after, swimming as though her life depended on it. That was another good thing. Tim loved dogs (one of his former girlfriends had told him he was very like a dog – affectionate but messy and annoying) and had missed having one in London. So it was fortuitous that Piggy had come into his life as soon as he moved into Lance's *gîte*. She was a black mongrel of some sort, a cross of what looked like Labrador and Collie. A proper dog that did proper fun doggy things like retrieve sticks, play football with her nose and swim. She also, he soon discovered, had a prodigious appetite, hence her new name.

She was just one of what appeared to be a shifting, ownerless population of dogs that roamed round the villages foraging for food. He supposed many of them did in fact have owners since they didn't look underfed but they were certainly not owned in the British sense of having a collar and a lead, a dog bowl and a home, if not a bed, they could call their own. Tim had yet to see a French dog being actually walked. They just walked themselves and slept outside wherever they happened to find themselves. There was one dog, a great shaggy thing like an Old English sheepdog, which made a habit of sleeping right in the middle of the main village street, seemingly unmoved by the cars that squealed round it, treating it like a traffic island.

Piggy had hung around his house from the day he moved in and once he had fed her, that was it – she was hooked and so was he. He had asked one or two neighbours if she belonged to anybody but they didn't know, and probably cared less. Now, two weeks on, she appeared to be a fixture who had readily adapted to a hearth and home, and that was fine by both of them.

Even at this time in the morning, the heat was intense and Tim drifted off. He had sat up late the night before working from home and felt he was owed some time off. Besides, he was looking forward to a swim and then he wanted to explore the *garrigue*. Tim had wondered at the name and had discovered it was Occitan, the medieval language of this part of France, for the small evergreen holm oaks which, together with other hardy bushes and aromatic plants, formed the wilderness that stretched as far as the eye could see. The scents of the *garrigue* were overpowering especially in the early morning and at night. It was like plunging into a huge *bouquet garni* and the sense of space was irresistible especially for anyone used to fighting for every inch in London.

Over the centuries in this part of France, many different people had made good use of the *garrigue* as a hiding place, from the persecuted Protestants who held their services in secret there, to the resistance fighters in the second world war who used the many caves to hide in. Of course the other creatures who made good use of the *garrigue* were the *sangliers* – the plentiful wild boar which apparently had a great time terrorising the odd walker or motorist throughout most of the year until October when hordes of French huntsmen came out of the woodwork and mass slaughter began.

A fly perched on Tim's nose and awoke him. Sitting up, he looked around for Piggy but couldn't see her. That was strange as she never went far away from him. She probably feared losing him more than he feared losing her. He stood up scanning the horizon, shouting for her and strolled round the part of the dam where one could swim. There was nobody around at this time on a weekday and the water was utterly still, the whole scene resembling nothing so much as a Scottish loch. After five minutes, Tim felt a pang of anxiety. Piggy wasn't the kind dog who would disappear after a scent like a terrier, especially now that she was fed regularly. Then his eyes focussed on the high concrete barrier which separated the part of the dam where you could swim from the huge expanse of water where it was forbidden, and below which millions of tons of water would fall down the walls when the dam was operative.

Drawing closer, he could see that there was access to the barrier up a stony walkway which was expressly forbidden to the public but was there for dam workers only. To his horror, looking up and shading his eyes from the relentless sun, he could now make out what seemed to be a silhouette of a dog up on the barrier; what was less clear was another shape beside it. They were right in the middle, with a vast drop on either side, and from where he was standing he couldn't make out if there was actually a walkway up there or just a ledge. Just then, the indeterminate shape stood up and Tim could see that it was a person – next to, he supposed, his dog. Christ, they could both fall at any moment. What the hell was going on?

He began to run towards the stony path that led vertically up to the barrier, not daring to shout in case he startled the dog into falling. As he reached the top he saw to his relief that what he assumed was just a ledge was in fact a proper walkway with low railings either side. Now the figure, whom he could see was in fact a young man, bent down and stroked the dog who was unmistakably Piggy, before leaning over the low railing at a dangerous angle. Then he put a foot on the lowest rung of the railing and looked as though he was about to climb over. My god, thought Tim, now on the walkway himself, it's a suicide.

'Hey', he cried, 'stop – stop for god's sake'. 'What the hell are you doing? STOP!' The young man, startled, turned towards him, jumped down on the walkway and slumped, sitting, against the rail. Piggy, recognising him, now ran up to greet Tim effusively and the young man – Tim could see he was only a teenager – turned to face him – a face so lost and stricken that Tim knew he had been right about the boy's intention to jump.

'I'm sorry', the boy said. 'Is this your dog? It followed me up here. Then it wouldn't go back.' Tim, struggling to catch his breath almost laughed with relief.

'It doesn't matter', he said. 'Are you all right? I thought you were going to jump….' Thank god the kid was English – how extraordinary, but at least he could talk to him. The boy started to sob, holding his face in his hands and rocking.

'I was', he moaned. 'I am… I would have done if the dog hadn't been here; I didn't want to leave her up here in case she fell… what's her name?'

'Piggy' said Tim. 'She's a stray I found. Thank god, she found you. Hey, come here…,' he put his arm round the boy. 'Come down below and let's talk about this… nothing can be so bad that you have to jump'.

The boy, wiping his face now with his hand, picked up a small backpack that he had with him and looked for a minute as though he might run. Tim's heart missed a beat. If the kid vaulted now over the railing, he might not be quick enough to stop him. Then, he seemed to think better of it, gave a little shrug and wiped his face again which was streaked with tears and grime. 'OK', he said. 'Maybe it was a lame idea.'

Vastly relieved, Tim led the three of them down the

stony track to the grassy bank where he had left his things. 'Listen', he said, when they had sat down on the rug he bought, 'you don't have to tell me what's wrong, but it might help to talk to a stranger. I'm a good listener and I also know how crap life can seem sometimes.' Ben sniffed and his eyes welled with tears again. To mask it, he reached out to stroke Piggy who had sat beside him and tried to put her head in his lap.

'Yeah,' he said. 'Maybe I should talk. Maybe that's been the problem that I haven't had anyone to talk to except my mum and I didn't want to make her anxious about me.' And then it all came out, the move from England, the loneliness, the unhappiness at school, the feeling that nothing would ever be right or fun again. It sounded so banal, Ben thought, the way he told it. It wasn't exactly an unusual story and it wasn't like he'd been tortured or something or lost all his family in a car crash, but it was a relief to talk and Tim, as the bloke had said his name was, seemed like a nice guy. He was nodding sympathetically and Piggy was now presenting him with sticks she had found so that he could throw them for her.

At that moment, there was squeal of tyres on the stony path leading to the dam and a car appeared causing a huge cloud of dust. Out of it leapt his mother and Judith Hay. Oh God, how did they know to come and look for him up here? They hadn't got his note yet because he'd only just written it up there on the bridge; it was in his bag. He stood up suddenly as Fern ran towards him with the surreal sense that he was in an action movie. She would embrace him and cry and demand explanations and he would… but at that point, his head swam and just like in the movie, the credits rolled and the screen went black. He passed out.

22

Much later when Tim finally got home, exhausted and shaken, he poured himself a drink and thought about the day that had started so promisingly. Ben, thank god, was fine. He had come round shortly after he fainted but Judith and Fern, took him to be checked out at the local hospital just in case he had taken an overdose of any kind. Tim hadn't needed to explain what was going on with Ben as the two women seemed to have sussed it. Perhaps he had left them a note. His mother had been hysterical, partly with the relief of Ben still being alive, partly because of what he had intended to do; the other woman, Judith, had been the calm one, taking stock of the situation and making all the decisions. When they had finally got Ben in their car, he had come to but wasn't making much sense. Tim had followed them in his own car to the hospital but had left soon afterwards since there was little he could do. He left his number with Judith and told them to call him to let him know how Ben was.

Fern called him later that afternoon once they were back at home. Ben had recovered well and was now at home with them. Would he like to come round, Fern asked hesitantly.

Ben had asked to see Tim in order to thank him for almost certainly saving his life. 'Of course I'll come over now,' replied Tim. 'But, Ben mustn't think I saved him. I don't think he wanted to jump really and Piggy provided him with a good excuse not to. Once he came down and talked to me, he seemed almost relieved. He told me how unhappy he'd been in France, especially at school, but I think even at that point, that he realised he'd got himself too worked up and lost touch with reality for a while.'

'I know', sniffed Fern who still couldn't stop crying. Though I blame myself for not seeing how bad it was for him. He just couldn't bear to talk to me about it all for fear of making me unhappy just when things were getting better. But of course now he doesn't have to go back to that school if he doesn't want to. That's the last thing that matters. And if he really wants to, we'll go back to England. I couldn't bear for him to be so miserable again. I must have been blind. I've been so busy trying to make a go of things here that somehow I just didn't notice how traumatic it's been for poor Ben.

But by the time Tim arrived and went to talk to him, Ben seemed almost cheerful. 'I'm sorry I put you through that. It's like I've been living in a nightmare for the past few weeks but I think it'll be OK now,' he told Tim. 'I've given myself a terrible shock as well as everyone else… Poor mum. She had no idea. Somehow I let it all get to me and then I found this website on the net which kind of encouraged people to end it all. I got talking to some of the others and they all got comfort from thinking they could end it all whenever they wanted. Some of them even want to make suicide pacts with you – you know, meet up and do it together. Mind you, they were pretty weird, most of them,' he added.

'Listen', said Tim, who now in some odd way felt responsible for Ben, 'I'm just really, really glad that I was there and from now on I'm sure things will improve. Your mum says you don't have to go back to that school and she's willing to move back to England too if necessary. But maybe now this has happened, you'll be able to cope better. Everything is more difficult in a foreign country and it takes much longer than you think to settle in. I haven't been here long and whilst I already love most things about being here, I admit it's been a bit lonely. I think you just need to make a few good friends and I'd like to be one of them if you let me. Just don't do anything dramatic again, and lose that website will you? If things continue to get you down, talk to me, first. Promise?'

Ben nodded. 'Sure,' he said. 'You've been great, and I'd love to take Piggy for walks sometimes. I've always wanted a dog'.

'You're on', said Tim. 'She was the one who stopped you jumping, after all.'

When he went downstairs, Fern, whom Tim desperately wanted to put his arms around, had finally stopped sobbing but still looked utterly stricken. Instead, being English, he left her his phone number and assured her that he would call the next day to see how things were and to help in any way he could.

'I can't thank you enough,' said Fern, biting her lip. 'I'm so sorry you had to spend your day this way. You were such a help. Please come round again – I know Ben would appreciate it.'

'Of course, I will. Tim smiled ruefully. 'I know today was horrendous for you, but for me it's been an opportunity to get to know you both. I'll do whatever I can for Ben – he's a good kid.'

'Don't worry, I'll stay with them tonight and look after them,' Judith said, emerging from the kitchen, as he turned to leave. 'But keep in touch. Ben clearly likes you and he needs some male companionship.'

There was something about Judith that Tim couldn't put his finger on. He hadn't taken her in properly throughout the events of the day, but when she said goodbye to him he knew that there was something very familiar about her. Could she have worked on his newspaper, or was she a friend of Freya's? She looked about her age. Or perhaps he'd seen her on telly? He must ask her when he saw her again. She had been brilliant today. Thank goodness Fern had her for a friend. It bugged him that he couldn't remember where he'd seen her before but he was too bloody tired to think about it. It'll come to me, he thought. The face he really wanted to dwell on, he realised with interest, was Fern's.

23

The night that Lance and Roland chose to go to their 'special interests club' in Montpellier was particularly hot and oppressive. The city was heaving with tourists and students and every outside-bar and café was packed. In the main square, Place de la Comédie, impromptu bands of musicians vied with each other to produce the most offensive noise and the usual gangs of doped out crusties with their dogs on rope leads draped themselves over every available fountain edge and all the way up the steps leading to the theatre itself. In front of the cinema complex, a troupe of jugglers and trick cyclists had drawn an admiring crowd while the usual sad man covered from top to toe in gold paint, cat perched on his shoulder, stood statue-like on a plinth at the entrance to the shopping mall, his gold top hat displaying the wretchedly few copper coins he garnered there every day of the year for his trouble.

Roland blagged his way to a table at the Café de la Paix facing the melee and immediately ordered two beers, the French waiters as usual pointedly ignoring the prior claims to tables or drinks of the foreigners who made up most of the clientele. 'We can't go to the club till ten,' he told Lance, 'so we may as well have a few beers first'.

Lance glanced at his watch. It was only 8.30. His shirt was already sticking to him and he felt grubby and slightly nauseous. Montpellier invariably had that effect on him at night. It was too bloody noisy and squalid, especially here in the Comédie. He studied a group of Arabs loitering near their table arguing with a couple of western students while another student doubled over the gutter vomiting. Doubtless some bicker over drugs. Really, it was like Dante's circle of hell here what with all these performing monkeys and low life prowling around. If it wasn't for the delights that Roland had promised him that night, he'd go home right now. In a rare moment of nostalgia, he imagined himself back in London in the coolly civilised surroundings of his club, summoning George – they were all called George in Boodles – for a large scotch.

Reluctantly, he turned his attention back to Roland who was sweating unattractively into his Hawaiian-style polyester shirt and exchanging shouted remarks with a man at a nearby table. Why couldn't they keep the noise level down in France, Lance thought irritably, his head pounding.

Just then he noticed a couple taking a table at the next door café. Well, well, if it wasn't Miss goody two shoes Judith Hay with that surly bastard Gerald Thornton. Of course, they would have met through their shared love of 'literature'. Lance saw the word in inverted commas because he was conscious that Gerald especially did not feel his own work was deserving of the term. Well, they deserved each other; each as pretentious as the other. Not that he'd be getting much joy from her – Tim Lavery had mentioned in the bar the other night that he had met Judith and finally recognised her from a newspaper story he had covered in England as being sacked from a girls' school for suspected hanky panky with the headmistress.

Lance had been so clearly thrilled with this spicy piece of news that Tim had quickly shut up about it, realising that his innocent indiscretion might be used by somebody as malicious as he now perceived Lance to be. In fact, when he saw how Lance had gloated, saying he knew there was 'something fishy' about her and that would make people think twice before befriending her, Tim had inwardly cursed himself. He liked what little he knew of Judith and she was a good friend to Fern; he was mortified to think how his careless remark might now affect her standing in the community.

When Judith noticed Lance only feet away from her, she said something to Gerald and they quickly moved off before ordering. Good riddance, thought Lance. I don't want them nosing around wondering what I'm doing here with Roland. Montpellier was a bit too small for his liking. You invariably bumped into somebody you knew sooner or later.

After Judith had asked Gerald if they could move because of Lance, she felt she owed him an explanation. Finding a small bar in a backstreet, she ordered a *pastis* and lit up a cigarette feeling distinctly wobbly. She hadn't seen the bastard since Rose had told her the shocking story of how Lance had attempted to rape Sophie. It was very much on her conscience and after agonising about what to do with this unwelcome information, she still hadn't come to any conclusion. Sophie wasn't there to talk to and it would be unpardonable, she felt, to tell Jean who was already in a dreadful state about Lance. In any case, it was, as yet, just unsubstantiated rumour and she knew all about that and the heartbreak it could cause.

However, now she found she felt she could at least confide in Gerald. She had attended a few poetry events at Wuthering Heights since their first meeting and she had been pleased and flattered that he had suggested going for a meal after today's book launch. She liked what she knew of him very much and was looking forward to getting to know him better. Instinctively, she felt he was a man she could trust with her dilemma. It was driving her crazy keeping the knowledge to herself.

In the event, she didn't have to bring the subject up. Gerald steered her to a chair and looked concerned. 'What is the matter?' he asked her. 'You look so shaken. I can understand you not wanting to join that bore Lance Campion for a drink, but we didn't have to flee in terror did we?'

Judith stubbed out her cigarette and took a gulp of *pastis*. Funny how that warm, aniseed taste was so soothing here in France; it wouldn't occur to you to drink the stuff in England. She took a deep breath and looking fixedly down at her glass told him what she knew of Lance from both his wife and from Rose. He didn't interrupt. When she had finished, she raised her eyes to his dreading to see disbelief or contempt. He'll think I'm just a hysterical gossip, she thought.

But Gerald put his hand over her unsteady one and looked at her only with concern. 'My God,' he said. 'You poor girl, carrying that around. I'm so glad you've been able to tell me about this. It's absolutely appalling if it's true. We must think what the best thing is to do. It's such a serious allegation, and whilst I wouldn't put anything past that pompous shit, it would be terrible to spread false rumours.'

Meanwhile, in a scruffy alley near the railway station, the object of Gerald and Judith's discussion, loitered outside a black metal door covered with graffiti in a largely boarded up building wondering what the hell he had got himself into. Roland had telephoned his contact Gilles on his mobile and they were waiting for him to open up 'the club'. When Gilles, unbarred the door, looking comically like the North African gangster Lance supposed he was, he nodded offhandedly to Roland, ignored Lance, and led them up a crumbling wooden staircase littered with cigarette ends to another locked door which opened into an apartment. Once inside, he asked Roland for cash in advance and after counting the notes disappeared into a back room. 'Some club', said Lance to Roland. 'What happens now? He legs it with our money and we find our own way out?' Roland grinned.

'Calm down, my friend. Now he goes to find our new friends and then he leaves us. There are other rooms here where we make ourselves comfortable and have very good time. You wanted this, no?'

Lance didn't have time to answer before Gilles returned with two dark-haired girls who didn't look much over twelve who smiled at the men shyly and shook hands. 'Anya,' said Gilles in French, 'and Brita. They are from Slovakia. They will entertain you here. I will return at 12.00. There is beer and wine in the fridge. Offer the girls a drink.'

Lance felt his initial misgivings melt away. Both girls were pretty in a Slavic way and well developed. They obviously knew what they were here for and didn't seem at all alarmed. After all, this wasn't some child slave outfit. Gilles was clearly just a pimp but the girls probably were a great deal better treated here than they were in their own countries. Brita now passed him a glass of wine and sat herself down beside him. 'Cheers', he said clinking his glass with her own. 'Do you speak English?'

24

It was well past midnight when Gerald saw Judith to her car after a rather good seafood dinner at his local bistro and she set off back home. As she was tired, she decided to take the Beziers road back to Vevey rather than risk falling asleep on the auto route which became even more alarming at night with vast trucks thundering along, either from the Spanish border, or on their way to it. If you got stuck between two of them on one of the stretches where there were eternal roadworks and you were down to one lane, it was like a rollercoaster ride to hell. You had to keep up with their speed or they bore down on you, lights glaring and sometimes even sounding their terrifying horns threatening to hurtle through your back window. The hair-raising American film, Dual, always sprang to mind on these occasions – the one where the innocent motorist is pursued at breakneck speeds by a psychotic trucker along cliff top Californian highways.

Why were the French such suicidal drivers, Judith wondered. They must teach them that style of ferociously threatening tailgating when they took driving lessons. They all did it; it wasn't just the boy racers. Normally mild-mannered French housewives became demons behind the wheel and even the *auto-école* cars with their learner drivers cut you up at high speed and waited for a corner to overtake. No wonder this country boasted the highest rates of road deaths in Europe – and by a huge percentage. Nor were they deterred by the worrying number of poplar trees one saw standing like sentries on either side of endless straight country roads with flowers tied to their trunks in memory of another fallen Frenchman who had collided with one.

Even more spooky was a large notoriously dangerous roundabout with several exits that Judith now edged round, on which at least a hundred ghostly cut-out silhouettes of people were displayed in a silent throng, each one apparently representing ten real people who had met their untimely deaths at that junction. At night, in the purple shadows, they loomed up in a spectacularly sinister way, a terrible reminder of mortality, yet the French friends to whom Judith had mentioned this national failing merely shrugged as though it was to be expected. 'It's the way the French drive', they would say, almost with a hint of Gallic pride at their statistical achievement in this area. 'What can you do?'

But tonight Judith was less troubled by the cavalier culling of motorists on French roads than by her decision, taken after discussion with Gerald, to speak to Jean about Lance and what had happened to Sophie. The fact that Jean already suspected Lance of inappropriate behaviour with

Sophie helped. She probably didn't realise the extent of it though and it was going to be very difficult. Jean might well, with reason, tell her it was none of her business; on the other hand, Jean might confront Lance and somehow put a stop to his activities. Sophie, Judith gathered from Rose, was probably going to be all right; another victim might not be so lucky. Perhaps it was a cowardly way of shifting the burden of knowledge but she felt that it was better for Lance if someone close to him warned him off than that the police were involved. Not that that was a viable option. The local gendarmerie took a dim view of foreigners and their problems as it was; they would scarcely take any notice of an Englishman stabbed through the heart on their doorstep, let alone take any interest in his sexual proclivities.

Gerald had been understandably wary about this course of action but he could see how much Judith needed to feel she was doing something responsible. 'If he can do that to Sophie, he's probably tried it before and will try again', she argued. 'He's clearly a sexual predator and somebody's got to do something about it. Jean already knows something, I'm sure of it. When she came to ask me what I saw Lance doing in Vevey that made him so angry, she said something about the past… something that happened in the past to do with all this. She was distraught, Gerald. It's perhaps better that she learns the truth about him, if she doesn't already know it.'

Gerald had still been anxious. 'It's not your problem, Judith, and this is all heresay, don't forget.'

'What I witnessed in Vevey wasn't heresay,' Judith retorted. 'The man is a monster. I already feel guilty because I could have perhaps prevented Sophie going out alone with Lance to begin with; Rose told me he was planning it and I could have told Sophie's parents then. Although I don't suppose they'd have stopped her. They don't seem that concerned about her.

'It's a ghastly mess,' conceded Gerald. 'I just don't want you to get caught up in it all; it could turn very nasty.'

Judith felt a little glow inside her as she thought about this conversation on the way home. It was a long time since anybody had been concerned about her.

As she turned the corner finally into her street, she was so wrapped up in her thoughts that she didn't notice the freshly sprayed graffiti on the wall outside her house. 'GO HOME ENGLISH SCUM' it read.

25

Judith did not have long to wait before she saw Jean. The following morning she received a telephone call from Frank Partridge whose estate agency in Vevey had been daubed with red paint and anti-English slogans during the night. Not only that, but many of the English owned houses in the town and surrounding villages had also been targeted and defaced with graffiti. Frank was keen to call a meeting of expats to try to defuse the crisis and work out what to do. 'I've spoken to the Mayor of Vevey who is very concerned and he's agreed to meet us tonight in the library to try to sort this out', he said. 'We mustn't let this anti-English thing spiral out of control. It's probably just a couple of workmen who've been fleeced by some idiot like Bill Bailey and are taking it out on the rest of us. Come to think of it I must phone Bill now and see if he's been affected up at the "manor". He's the one I won't feel sorry for, if so.'

Judith's first rather uncharitable thought was relief that she hadn't been singled out for abuse. Her next was the old familiar feeling of fear and insecurity. It would be awful if she were to be drummed out of France, just as she felt she had been from England. Finally, she was beginning to feel settled and content here in La Prairie, especially now that she had struck up a friendship with Gerald Thornton. A kindred spirit at last! She damn well wasn't going to move again just because of a little local hostility.

She could see that it must be infuriating in a way for the French in this improbable backwater to be so comprehensively invaded by the English – she didn't care for it herself – but on the other hand, the local economy benefited from it and villages like hers which had been dying on their feet were now thriving again thanks to foreign investors. In the past, young people couldn't get out fast enough to go and find work in the cities and virtually every small shop and business had closed down. Only the village bakers seemed to survive since the French needed their daily bread in the way the British need a pint in the pub.

She started to telephone the people Frank hadn't had time to call or didn't know. They needed as many people as possible at the meeting tonight. She thought of Fern and then hesitated. Fern didn't need another crisis in her life right now, but on the other hand, she would see the graffiti herself and be worried. Then she remembered Tim. He certainly should come to the meeting. As a journalist he might have some bright ideas as to how best to tackle this, and he could perhaps break the news gently to Fern. Jean would have the number of the *gîte* – and come to think of it, Jean and Lance would have to be there too. With any luck, Jean rather than Lance would answer the phone.

'I'm glad you've called,' Jean said when Judith got hold of her. 'Lance is spitting. His car has been vandalised which he thinks is all part of this anti-English thing. If it is, they certainly knew how to rile him the most. The house, thank god, seems to have escaped. Frank has already told him about the meeting and he's in his study now preparing some Churchillian war speech. Personally, I think it's a storm in a teacup – probably local kids. I've got more pressing concerns – as you know…', her voice faltered. In fact, Judith, I was wondering if I could talk to you again. I hope you don't mind, but you seem to be the only person I can think of confiding in.'

Judith paused. Fate seemed to have determined her course of action. She had to tell Jean what she knew now, but she'd see what Jean had to say first. 'Of course we can talk,' she told Jean. 'Why don't you come back to my place for a coffee after the meeting?'

In Tim's *gîte* the phone rang on the floor by his bed but the sound was almost completely muffled by a pile of discarded clothes and books topped by one of Piggy's many sticks that lay more or less on top of it. As it rang on, Judith wondered if he was still asleep since it was only just after eight, but even if Tim had been asleep, he probably wouldn't have heard it. In fact, Tim, unusually for him, was already striding along stony tracks through the nearby *garrigue* with Piggy in the lead swerving in and out of the thorny undergrowth in search of small animals and ever larger sticks for Tim to throw.

For Tim, as he put it to himself, was on a mission. Like his dog, he was onto the scent of something – and that something, he told himself, could possibly be a story. The newshound in him had not died even though it had been dormant for a while. Also money was becoming tight and Tim needed some fresh ideas for his column back in England.

The fact was that the previous day, whilst Tim had been out in the same area around dusk, a favourite time when the sun was setting in a red flush in the sky and the scents of the *garrigue* seemed to be at their strongest, he had suddenly caught sight of someone in the distance who every so often seemed to disappear into the ground and then emerge again. Intrigued, Tim moved a little closer until he could make out that the figure was a man hunched a little under the weight of whatever he was carrying, who did indeed seem to go down into the ground every so often. Instinctively, he stayed where he was not wanting to be seen but determined to investigate once the man had gone.

Some twenty minutes later, he heard a car being driven at speed along the track towards him throwing up clouds of dust and small pebbles. Grabbing Piggy by her collar, he crouched behind some gorse bushes as it went past, peering out just enough to establish that the driver was Roland, the café owner's son, in his ancient blue Renault van.

What the hell was he doing up here, he wondered. The only people he had ever encountered before were the one or two old farmers who still eked out a living by tending small hillside vineyards that they had somehow coaxed out of the inhospitable territory. And why did he keep doing that disappearing act? He started to walk in the direction he had seen Roland but by then it was getting dark – something that seemed to happen more suddenly than it did at home – and he had several miles to cover. Reluctantly he turned back, but not before noting some markers in the landscape so that he could find the spot again. I'll come back early in the morning, he thought, when I can be sure that Roland will be working in the café and nobody else should be about. He was sure Roland was up to no good in the *garrigue*. The man was a shifty looking bastard, he thought, who virtually snarled at anyone he didn't know who walked into his café. Or perhaps it was just the English interlopers he didn't like, with the exception of Lance who, strangely, appeared to be his best buddy. And that wasn't much of a recommendation.

Now in the early morning light, with a light breeze blowing in from the sea, Tim paused to get his bearings. Nobody was around which was good – but he couldn't quite recall the exact area where Roland had been foraging around. He started climbing up from the path towards a clump of rock roses which he thought he recognised and went on stumbling around amongst the thorny bushes for another half a mile or so. It was Piggy who alerted him to the spot he wanted – or rather Piggy's disappearance. Where on earth had she got to?

Ten minutes of increasingly frantic whistling and calling later, Tim heard scrabbling and rustling to the left of him and the dog ran into view, shaking mud off herself. 'Where the hell have you been?' Tim asked her, relieved that she wasn't stuck down some rabbit burrow. She was completely filthy – she must have been digging. He turned in the direction Piggy had come from and then all became clear. Partially concealed by branches and undergrowth that had been recently moved out of the way was the entrance to a cave. That would explain both Piggy's appearance and Roland's disappearance. Now he came to think of it, Tim knew that there were many such caves in the *garrigue* which had been put to all kinds of clandestine uses throughout history. The question was, what use was Roland Rat putting it to?

Wishing he had a torch, Tim cautiously made his way into the relatively narrow entrance of the cave. It was pitch black and very wet and muddy but after several metres, the tunnel opened out and thanks to a chasm in the rock roof above him which let in some light, Tim could make out dozens of wooden crates. His eyes adjusting to the light now he could see that they all contained bottles of wine – thousands of bottles in all, old and dusty. So that was Roland's game! He was some kind of wine smuggler. This little lot must be worth a fortune. But how and why had he come across it? He certainly wouldn't have been able to afford to buy such quantities, and even if he had, he would hardly be storing them in the middle of nowhere. Clearly, this was stolen booty. Roland must have been removing a couple of cases of it yesterday.

All of Tim's newspaper instincts were on red alert. Carefully he removed a couple of bottles which wouldn't be immediately noticed and put them in the rucksack he used to carry water. And now, he thought, I'm going to leg it before Roland comes back for more. He didn't fancy his chances if that weasel-faced little shit caught him here red-handed.

26

The meeting was held in Vevey Bibliothèque, the town's library, the staff there being quite accustomed to large numbers of British people using their facilities which, in most cases, were considerably better than in their own home towns. A private room had been booked by Frank Partridge who was to address the meeting. Many of tonight's participants were familiar with it since it was the room where an unappealingly bossy woman called Heather held a monthly bookclub meeting that which had started off with about 25 members but was now down to about 10, owing partly to Heather's overbearing personality, and partly because she forced them all to read obscure French literary works when they wanted only to discuss the likes of *Captain Corelli's Mandolin*. The bookclub had announced that it was open to all comers, English and French alike but, as usual, in any co-operative venture, only English people had shown up.

Judith had been approached by Heather shortly after arriving in La Prairie – 'You'll be a splendid addition to the group', Heather had said, 'with your background in literature. I'm afraid some of our members are a little lax in their reading habits. I'm all for self-improvement, aren't you?' Wisely, Judith had prevaricated, not wishing to offend, but also not desperately wanting to be told what to read by the harridan Heather. 'What did she used to do in Britain?' she asked Camilla Stanhope one day. 'Oh, I think she was a tax inspector', said Camilla. 'Priceless, isn't it? Did you notice her moustache?'

Now, quarter of an hour before the meeting began, Heather was the first person Judith saw as she came into the room, sitting in the front row of chairs that had been put out, flanked by a couple of her book club stalwarts. Quickly acknowledging them, Judith hurried on to the back where she spotted some less threatening companions. Lance, she saw, was also in place near the front, importantly rustling some papers – a harrumphing speech no doubt. He glanced up at her as she passed and managed a frosty greeting. Judith's stomach turned somersaults. All she could think of was that he should be behind bars; she really must pass on the information about him that she had. She only wished that it didn't have to be to his poor, downtrodden wife who sat beside him and smiled wanly at Judith. 'See you later', mouthed Judith when Lance's back was turned. Jean nodded and fumbled in her handbag for her specs.

The room filled up suddenly and more chairs had to be hurriedly squeezed in. Many people, apparently, had been affected by the recent spate of anti-British feeling, and those who hadn't been were apprehensive as to what might be coming. Sue, the tennis coach, complained loudly that some of her French pupils had abruptly cancelled lessons with her. 'It's ridiculous,' she exclaimed. 'There's just a few people whipping up this anti-Brit thing but it seems to be catching on fast. I'm beginning to feel like a Jew in pre-war Germany.' This was received with a few nervous giggles. Trust Sue to go too far, thought Judith. She really was a silly woman.

Frank Partridge called the meeting to order and introduced the Mayor of Vevey, known to many there who had met him at other Anglo-French functions. M. Berol, was a charming, educated man who spoke English fluently and was fully aware of the economic benefits accruing from the town's fast growing British community. He gave a short speech designed to quell fear and proffer reassurance. 'This is the work of a small minority of French people,' he said 'who, I think, are not against the British in themselves, but mistakenly think that they will somehow 'take over' in this part of France. They feel vulnerable because young people cannot find work here, cannot therefore afford housing here and move to the cities. The foreigners find the houses cheap and the sense of community especially in some villages, they feel, is lost.

'However, most people realise that the foreigners who come here do only good. They restore houses which would otherwise fall into decay; they spend money locally; they employ local workmen and they tell me they like it here. They move here for the peace, the countryside, the quality of life and so on; they do not wish to spoil it for us; quite the reverse.

'I know this, and I say to you: put your faith in us. We will find the people responsible for the current spate of vandalism and they will be punished. Do not be driven away from this beautiful part of France. We welcome you here and we want you to stay'.

M. Berol was applauded politely but he had no experience of the British when their hackles have risen. A phlegmatic race, to be sure, but not when their property was threatened. The French, it had been explained to Judith, did not bother about the outside appearance of their property – 'We hide our wealth and our good taste within', one decorator had told her. 'We do not want to be accused of showing off to our neighbours.'

Consequently, it was feared, the mayor would not understand that offensive graffiti on their outside walls and car bonnets was no small matter for the British. It struck at their very hearts, especially since so many of them had been to all the trouble and expense of repainting and plastering their houses. The French-owned ones, however prosperous the inhabitants, always looked as though they were about to fall down. Nor was the kindly mayor prepared for the kind of grilling he was about to get in the question and answer session that followed his short speech. Feelings were running high and the British were used to a rather higher level of both democratic discussion and public accountability than their friends across the Channel.

Both Lance and Bill Bailey vied with each other to pin down the mayor on exactly what action he planned to take before turning on each other. Swiftly, this deteriorated into a slanging match. 'It's people like you who give the British a bad name,' shouted Lance. 'You come here with pots of money, snap up a chateau from under French noses, employ a totally British workforce to put it right and then complain that you can't find anywhere to eat fish and chips. You have absolutely no sense of the history and culture of the place at all. Jim has just asked the mayor what we English can do to preserve the traditions and heritage of rural France. He was too polite to give you the correct answer, so I'll do it for him: bugger off back to Oldham. We don't want your sort here, and neither do the French.

'And I suppose they do want your sort here, do they?' asked Bill ominously. 'Pretentious twats in panama hats and posh voices who ogle underage girls. Don't think we haven't noticed that… you may be called a boulevardier here Mr Campion but back in Oldham we'd have other names for it.'

There was an agonised silence while the audience digested this. 'Please, please' said the Mayor, flapping his papers ineffectually. 'Let us not quarrel among ourselves'.… but nobody paid him any attention. Amid the groundswell of voices, Lance got to his feet: 'You'll be hearing from my solicitor', he said turning to Bill Bailey, his voice shaking with anger. 'You won't get away with this'… he began to walk out of the meeting, then remembered his wife: 'Are you coming Jean?' he asked furiously. But Jean, whose head had been bowed during the heated exchanges, now looked up at him. 'No, Lance, I'm not,' she said quietly.

Lance looked stunned and began to speak but then thought the better of it. He stalked out of the room, slamming the door behind him. My god, thought Judith. Bill Bailey has done my work for me… poor, poor Jean, but how remarkable that she's stood her ground. This will really set the cat among the pigeons.

The meeting resumed after much coughing and shuffling but at a more subdued level. Several people stood up to complain that the French were being unfair given that the British had actually increased the available housing stock with their love of DIY and renovation. The French, they pointed out are happy to offload their old houses and barns, often leaving them to rot, however historic, and move to new bungalows or flats in the suburbs; the British did them up to make them habitable then either lived in them themselves, boosting the local economy, or sold them on. Others pointed out that apart from the building trade, the wine growers had reason to thank the expatriates. 'We drink a damned sight more local wine than the locals', said one.

Others pointed out that it was all very well boosting the local economy; what their French friends told them, they said, was that the British failed to integrate. Some spoke French, or at least tried to; an astonishing number didn't even try. 'That's ridiculous,' cried Sue, the tennis coach. 'Whenever I try to speak French in a local shop or something, they always pretend they can't understand and look at me as if I'm something the dog brought in. Many of the locals are frankly contemptuous of us. I don't know what the answer is.

'Go back to Britain,' someone said in a loud whisper, but Sue's ears, were like satellite stations. 'I heard that', she retorted, glaring in the general direction it came from. 'Believe me, I would go back if I could afford to. I'm afraid, like many people here, I've burned my boats financially. I can't afford to go back to Britain.' This was greeted by rumbles of assent. Then one of Frank Partridge's rival estate agents in the town (there were now more than 20 thanks to the foreign influx) spoke up: 'Most of the anti-British feeling here actually comes from other Brits,' he said. 'I get Brits who say to me, 'Oh, I don't want a British neighbour'.'

'I'm afraid that's right,' Judith whispered to her neighbour. 'It's also a snobbish thing. People don't mind Lady Bracknell moving in down the road, but they object to a plumber from Birmingham… it wouldn't surprise me if the perpetrator of all this graffiti came from Godalming.'

27

'My god, you don't know what you've missed,' Fern told Tim in a low voice as he slipped into the seat she had saved for him, out of breath and furious with himself for missing the beginning of the meeting. This whole affair promised to make a good story for the *Sunday Times*. She filled him in on the Lance-Bill exchange as one after the other angry British residents stood up to tell the mayor about the damage they had suffered and to demand recompense. Shit, thought Tim when she came to the part about underage sex, better make it the *Sunday Sun*.

The mayor looked deeply uncomfortable as he listened to the catalogue of woe: Several people had awoken to find 'English go home' sprayed on their car bonnets or walls of their businesses. Others had had their tyres slashed and matchsticks jammed into car door locks. One main street in Vevey named after the French economist Jean Monnet had been scathingly dubbed Rue d'Anglais by the locals. Clearly the *Entente Cordiale* was crumbling fast.

Frank Partridge tried to bring order to the meeting. 'Of course I deplore what has happened to many of us,' he said, 'but perhaps this is a wake-up call for us to behave with, let's just say a little more tact in future as a community. You can understand some of the locals feeling that their neighbourhoods have been overrun. We must do our best to integrate – and that means learning the language and doing things the French way if we want to remain on good terms with our neighbours.

'Does it also mean you not selling any more French houses to the British at such inflated prices that the locals can't afford 'em? Jeered Bill Bailey. 'Come off it Frank. The real problem round here is that house prices have risen by about 15 per cent this year – and whose fault is that? You damn estate agents, that's who!'

'It also didn't help when you came along with your pots of money and snaffled up the major house in the area from under the noses of genuine French *vignerons*', added Heather, getting to her feet, her face scarlet with annoyance. 'At least most of us try to keep a low profile and don't go round demanding a sizzling English breakfast at local cafes!'

'Oh, stop bellyaching, love, and get back to your books,' retorted Bill, enjoying himself now. 'At least I've brought business to this area. What have you done for it? What have any of you done for it, come to that? You come down here full of middle class self-righteousness to live in a medieval time-warp, thinking you're oh-so-continental because you buy a few olives every now and then, and paint your shutters blue, but you're just a bloody nuisance as far as the natives are concerned. No wonder they're pissed off. Just be thankful that they haven't yet done what they're famous for in these parts and begun a massacre. Come to think of it, this is probably the lead-up to it. What you need to get in your heads is that as far as they're concerned here it's permanent payback time. As for me, I'm getting out of this shit-hole and moving to Spain which is a lot friendlier – and has better grub.'

'Good riddance', shouted Heather, beside herself. 'Best place for you. You'll feel at home on the Costa del Sol. It's full of nobodies from Oldham like you!'

Frank stood up. 'Please, everybody, this is not helpful. We don't want to fight a civil war, as well as Agincourt, all over again. I suggest we ask the Mayor to say a few more words and then call this meeting to a close. If any of you have any sensible suggestions about what's going on, please see me afterwards and we'll form a committee to work on them.'

The meeting ended soon afterwards in some disarray. 'Blimey,' said Tim to Fern, 'this beats covering Kensington and Chelsea council meetings. What a cracking story for the Sunday papers!' Fern giggled, but she looked anxious all the same. 'Oh Tim, I don't want to have to go back to Britain now', she said. 'Just when everything is going so well and Ben is beginning to really enjoy himself again. Did you know he'd been seeing that girl Rose Evans? Judith introduced them and they've become really good friends. It makes such a difference.'

Tim looked at her affectionately. 'Hey, don't worry, Ferny', he said, squeezing her hand. 'This is just a little local difficulty, you'll see. We're not going to be drummed out of here just because of a handful of bored youths. Besides, I can't leave yet; I think I'm onto a really big story.'

Lance didn't trust himself to get into his car. His heart was thumping painfully in his chest, his head had started to ache and his clothes were sticking to him uncomfortably. He had suffered a nasty shock at the meeting, only compounded by his own wife showing solidarity with that rabble by refusing to walk out with him. Furiously, he walked to a bar in one of the back streets of Vevey where he slipped anonymously into a table at the back and nursed a whisky. He couldn't risk going to Roland's at this point; first, he didn't want to be seen being too chummy with him in case Roland's proclivities had become known too; and second, for all he knew it was that unpleasant father of his who was drumming up all the anti-British stuff that was going on. He hadn't felt too comfortable in there lately, noticing the hostility that seemed to radiate from the small gangs of blue-overalled peasants that passed the time of day in there. He didn't think Roland could be part of it, but you never knew. The French were treacherous buggers.

Grimly, he tried to think logically about Bill Bailey's barely concealed threats. How could he possibly have found out about Sophie, assuming that was what he was on about. He was pretty sure she wouldn't have blabbed about what had happened. And he couldn't know about the night in

Montpellier, could he? He had to have seen him with Sophie at some point… or… shit, of course. There was one person who could have spread gossip about him, who was malevolent enough and who had, unfortunately seen him that market day with Sophie. That bloody interfering prissy schoolteacher. He'd been right to take against her from the beginning. Still, she could talk.

Thanks to Tim, he knew now what she was running away from and where her own interests lay. It shouldn't be too much of a problem to get hold of the newspaper cuttings on her untimely exit from The Chase. That would cook her goose all right! It might also serve to deflect any shit flying in his direction. He could easily say that she had been lying about him because he knew her repellent little secret. In another age she'd have been burnt as a witch. With that comforting thought, Lance downed another whisky and set off for home. Now to tackle Jean. How dare she humiliate him like that? Was the woman completely out of her mind? She too would be shortly be very, very sorry.

28

But Jean wasn't at home when Lance slammed in shouting for her. She and Judith were sitting at Judith's kitchen table sharing a bottle of wine. Jean was visibly upset and yet managed to keep any tears at bay. What had happened at the meeting had confirmed her fears about Lance. Bill Bailey had practically accused him publicly of being a pervert; evidently, it was common knowledge that he liked young girls. But oddly this confirmation of her suspicions had given her new resolve. A week ago, she would never have dared to defy Lance in the way she had – even in private, let alone in public. But his public humiliation had given her strength; it was an unfamiliar feeling, scary, and yet satisfying. She pushed her empty glass towards Judith who offered her. 'Thanks,' she said gratefully. 'I needed this. That meeting was dreadful. What Bill Bailey said about Lance was so… terrible and so unexpected. Have I been completely blind? Does everybody know what he's been up to? I can't bear it, I feel such a fool and so angry. What on earth will I do now, Judith? How can I face him?'

Judith gripped her glass tightly. It was now or never. She had to tell Jean what she knew. Thank god, in a way, it wasn't going to come as a complete surprise any more. 'You were great, tonight, Jean,' she said. 'It must have taken a lot of courage to sit tight when Lance flounced out – and it was the right thing to do because it's important now that you distance yourself from him however hard that's going to be. I – I hate to be the bearer of even more bad news but I feel I have to add now to what you already know. It's been on my conscience and since you already know now what Lance is like around young girls, perhaps it won't come as such a terrible shock….'

Judith hesitated. 'Go on,' Jean said grimly. 'If there's anything else I ought to know, please tell me now. It's important… more important than you think.'

'Well, if you're sure,' began Judith. 'It's something Rose Evans told me. She heard it directly from Sophie Stanhope and didn't know what to do about it even though Sophie had sworn her to secrecy. It's a terrible story, Jean, and you can choose not to believe it if you want, but I have to say that I do believe Rose. She had no reason to lie to me….'

'What is it? For God's sake tell me,' whispered Jean.

Judith took a gulp of wine. 'Lance tried to rape Sophie', she said quietly. 'He took her out to dinner by the beach and got her drunk. Then he became violent with her on the beach. I'm not sure how far it went because Sophie herself became hysterical. She said he had to stop because they were disturbed by other people on the beach but she was very shaken and bruised according to Rose. He told her that she mustn't tell anybody, and that if she did nobody would believe her because they all knew what a fantasist she was. She was terrified apparently.'

'Oh my god,' moaned Jean. Her face was drained of colour. 'Oh that poor child.' She slammed her glass on the table. 'How could he? How could he do that? This is so much worse than I thought.' She put her head in her hands and started to cry.

Judith cast around helplessly for something comforting to say but didn't come up with anything. She put her hand on Jean's. 'I'm sorry,' she whispered. 'I'm so sorry.'

'What did Sophie tell her parents?' Jean asked finally. 'Surely she said something?'

'Apparently not. She covered up her bruises and they didn't notice anything. You know what they're like – not overly concerned with her. They were flying back to England the next day and Sophie went straight back to school. She didn't tell anyone until she saw Rose and then she broke down and told her the whole story. Rose told her she must report it, but she wouldn't. I think she just wanted it all to go away and she must have felt that nobody would believe her. After all, she did flirt with Lance at that barbeque. In a way, she led him on, but of course she didn't expect it to end up like that.'

Jean was silent for a moment. Tears had given way to anger. 'She must tell someone', she said. 'Nobody should have to suffer that in silence. If she won't tell anyone, you must tell her parents, Judith. The terrible thing is, I believe her. I believe that Lance is capable of that. He drinks and gets into violent rages – out of control. He's frightening like that – I've seen it. The worst of this is that I have been a sort of collaborator in all this. I've never stood up to him, never crossed him. I was scared of him, scared of his temper and his sarcasm. And as for his liking young girls for sex – I think I knew about it; I think I've always known about it. I was very young when he married me, you know. He only was interested in me for a couple of years sexually. I suppose I got too old for him….'

'Are you sure you want to take this any further?' asked Judith. 'I don't feel it's really up to me to tell Sophie's parents. I think somebody ought to talk to Sophie first. It might just make it more traumatic for her to have to tell anyone. I don't know what to do for the best. I knew I'd have to tell you, but after that, I haven't been able to decide what's for the best. I mean, Lance should be stopped, I can see that, but perhaps, to be fair to him, it was just a one-off. You know Sophie looks older than she is and she was very flirtatious with him. You can't expect an older man not to be flattered. He probably thought she was keen on him whereas I imagine she was just showing off to Rose – that's what Rose thinks anyhow.'

Jean pushed back her chair and walked over to the window. For a few moments she stood looking out in silence. Then she turned round. 'It wasn't a one-off,' she said. 'I think he may have raped our daughter.'

29

It wasn't until the next day that Tim was able to start following up his wine scoop. Fern had been agitated when he told her about it and touchingly worried on his account. 'Please be careful,' she had said over dinner after the meeting. 'First this anti-Brit thing and now you seem to have stumbled across something that could land you in deep trouble. You don't want to antagonise Roland and his cronies. I don't like the look of him or his beetle-browed father – or any of that gang which hangs around at that place all day. They all radiate hostility; I wouldn't be surprised if it was they who were orchestrating this campaign against us.'

'Fern, I appreciate your concern, but this could lead to something really big,' said Tim. 'I'll be careful, I promise, but you must see how important this could be. Roland is clearly up to no good and I can't tell you how astonishing that great stash of old wine is up on the *garrigue*. It's got to be stolen – or why is it there?'

'Why don't you show the bottles you took to someone who knows about wine?' asked Fern. 'There may be some perfectly reasonable explanation for it. I know, what about asking Alan Knight? He's a retired wine auctioneer and expert– he was telling me at one of those barbeques that that was the reason he was down here. He was some big shot in London specialising in French wine and he got to love it so much around here that he moved down here permanently when he retired.'

'Brilliant idea', said Tim. 'I will. I was trying to think of someone I could ask about wine other than my pompous know-it-all brother-in-law who would delight in lecturing me. Alan is bound at least to know someone I could ask.'

He looked fondly over at Fern who grinned back at him. 'Perhaps I should have been a journalist too,' she said. 'Don't even think of it,' said Tim. 'You're far too nice. I like you just the way you are. You should have seen all those hatchet-faced hackettes I used to work with.

'But not the hatchet-faced hacks?' Fern asked.

'I wasn't hatchet-faced enough', replied Tim. 'Funny thing is, now I'm here, I'm much more keen to sniff out stories. I think being a freelance suits me.' They smiled uncertainly at each other. Their friendship had been cemented in the past few weeks since Ben's failed suicide bid. Neither of them had pushed it further but both of them felt that an affair was not out of the question. Tim now leaned towards Fern and kissed her gently on the mouth. 'You're lovely, you know', he said. 'I feel very protective towards you which is a pretty unfamiliar feeling for me. All the women I've known have wanted to boss me around. You're quite different, thank god.'

'I'm glad', said Fern. 'I'm quite keen on being protected at the moment. Hearing about what has happened to other people recently has made me nervous. I'm not sure I'll sleep at all well tonight.'

'Would it help if I stayed with you?' asked Tim a shade too promptly. Fern couldn't help smiling.

'It might', she said.

Next morning, after bidding Fern a tender farewell and high-fiving Ben on the stairs, Tim sought out Alan Knight clutching his two bottles in a plastic bag. He reckoned he'd just show them to Alan to see what he thought before telling him how he'd come by them.

Alan was gratifyingly intrigued. 'Most of the label has disintegrated', he told Tim, 'but you can just make out a word or two – look, '*…oide*' there and what looks like '*…lang*' there. Clearly French, clearly old –in fact, looking at the type of bottles and corks, I would say 1940 vintage –something like that. War time probably. Where did you get these?'

Tim hesitated, but decided to rely on Alan's discretion. After all, he rather needed his help. 'Let's just say, for the moment, that I found them,' he said, in the countryside, along with hundreds of others, not far away. It's obviously a hidden stash, and I know who's involved in it, but I'd rather not tell you that at the moment. For all I know, it's perfectly above board, but I somehow I doubt it.'

Alan looked thoughtful. 'Do you know anything about what happened in the south of France during the war on the wine front?' he asked. Tim shook his head. 'Nope. Never thought about it.'

'Well, this may help clarify things,' said Alan. 'During the German occupation of France, the Third Reich wanted to get their hands on France's fine wines and huge amounts were stolen from wine estates and restaurants all over France'. 'What did they do with it?' asked Tim.

'Well, for one thing, they drank it. Although Hitler himself didn't care for wine – he called it 'vulgar vinegar', many of the Nazi top brass, especially Goring and Goebbels, possessed vast collections of wine in Germany. Ribbentrop's preference was for champagne, I believe. He represented a couple of the famous champagne houses in France before the war and even married into the business. Goring was famous for sending military trucks to various wine estates, especially in Bordeaux, with no official authorization or anything, to haul away masses of wonderful wine for his personal collection. And what they didn't drink, they took back to Germany to sell internationally – it helped finance the war'.

'I had no idea,' said Tim. 'Couldn't the wine growers do anything to stop them?'

'They tried to hide the stuff from the Germans. Many of them built false cellar walls and that kind of thing. But it was largely impossible. The Germans had recruited teams of wine experts who knew the growers in France and knew just what stock they had. The French called them '*Weinführers*' – they sniffed out the wine and bought huge quantities – compulsorily purchased in many cases – to send back to Germany. Sometimes the French co-operated with them willingly of course; it was often worth their while.'

'So you think this hoard I've found could date back to the war?' asked Tim?

'In all probability. It looks the right kind of age, and why else would it be hidden in the countryside?'

Tim whistled. 'This is going to be big!' he exclaimed. 'Alan, you must help me. How can I best find out exactly what's going on?'

Alan thought for a moment. 'I've got a friend in the business I could ask,' he said. 'He's a wine grower over towards Beziers – one of those old aristocrats whose family have been in it for generations; in fact, he was one of the reasons I came to this area. I used to auction wine for Christies and did a lot of business with him… I could ask him, if you like. He may be able to recognise these bottles.'

'That would be a good start,' said Tim. 'Thank you so much, Alan. I'd better tell you all that I know about all this. I think there's something really fishy going on.'

30

Lance was already asleep by the time Jean returned from Judith's house. She had deliberately waited until it was late so as to avoid an unpleasant scene. When she quietly let herself in, the house reeked of cigar smoke and stale alcohol. Lance had evidently coped with the aftermath of the meeting in time-honoured fashion by laying into the whisky and feeling sorry for himself. Had she been around, he would have laid into her too. He must have been livid with her for abandoning him like that. But, having spoken to Judith and, for the first time, openly acknowledged her fears about what Lance may have done to Sarah, she had made up her mind. She was going to London first thing in the morning to renew her search for Sarah and to get away from Lance. The thought of staying a minute longer with him repelled her. She was not going to live with a child molester – and what's more – she was going to find out if that was what had driven her daughter away. How could she have been so blind and so stupid? How could her first loyalties have been to her repugnant husband instead of her child? Overcome with remorse, she decided that she would stay in London until she had found Sarah. And if she discovered that he had touched her, or harmed her in any way, she would avenge her – of that she was now absolutely sure.

Meanwhile, she had to pack a few things without Lance waking up and as soon as it was light, she was going to walk over to the bus stop. She didn't think she'd have any difficulty getting on the Ryanair flight the next evening from Montpellier. She would leave Lance a note saying simply that she was taking a break in England. She didn't think he'd make much of an effort to find her.

She tiptoed up the stairs. The bedroom door was ajar and Lance was lying on his back snoring across the whole bed. A floorboard creaked and he stirred. 'Jean?' he muttered. She froze, and after a few seconds he turned over and went back to sleep. Quickly she got together some basics for the journey – fortunately, she kept most of her clothes in a spare room where she was going to spend what remained of the night. One thing she must do, however, before she left. She padded silently down to Lance's study and inched open the door which creaked. Once inside, she opened the drawer where she had tucked away the photograph she'd found of Sarah and her friend Louise posing topless on the beach. If she couldn't track down Sarah straight away, at least she could try to find Louise.

Back upstairs, she climbed into the single bed, curled up and drew the covers round her. The night was hot and the room was airless, but she felt cold and panicky. She lay there, muscles clenched, listening to her heart thud and wondering if she would ever feel happy again. How could she ever forgive herself? Finally, she slept.

It was after ten thirty in the morning before Lance came to himself. The sun streaming through the slats in the shutters woke him – that, and a splitting headache. Instantly, the mortifying events of the previous evening came back to him. What the fuck was Bill Bailey on about? He would bloody sue him for slander – insinuating in the meeting in front of everybody that he was some kind of pervert. It was fucking intolerable. And, just as bad, was Jean refusing to walk out with him –as if she were in agreement with Bill. Recalling that, he sat up in bed and yelled for her. No reply. Where the fuck was she? He'd never forgive her. 'Jean,' he bellowed. 'Where the hell are you?' Shouting made his head throb more. Throwing on a towelling robe, he went to the bathroom and then made his way downstairs. She was probably in the garden, damn her. On his way to the fridge to get some juice he spotted a note on the table.

'Gone to London for a while', he read. What the devil… ? No explanation; no forwarding address. What the hell was she up to? Instinctively, he walked towards the phone, then he remembered. Jean didn't bloody have a mobile. Of course, she wouldn't. That was the kind of antediluvian idiot she was. Too bloody complicated and modern for her he supposed. Well, she could fuck off for all he cared. Good bloody riddance in fact. He might have wrung her neck if he had seen her this morning, staring at him with those watery, reproachful eyes. A thought struck him. Surely she didn't suspect him of anything? He'd been so careful, and Jean just wasn't the type to think ill of anybody. Anyway, even if she did, what could she do? She was a useless bitch. He doubted whether she would even be able to find her way to London on her own. Shaking his head at her stupidity, he climbed the stairs again back to bed, took some paracetamol and fell back to sleep.

Scarcely an hour later, he was woken up again by the persistent ring of the phone next to the bed which drilled into his consciousness. 'Yes?', he barked into the receiver thinking it must be Jean. 'Where the hell are you?'

'I'm at home,' said Tim, puzzled. 'It's me, Tim.'

'What is it?' said Lance testily. 'I'm asleep.'

'Sorry', said Tim. 'It's 11.30 though. It's just that I'm writing a piece for the paper about the anti-English business and I wanted a quote from you.'

'Oh, for God's sake,' exploded Lance. 'I'm so damn fed up with all of this. Why can't you get quotes from the sodding French? It's them that's got some explaining to do.'

'Well, I shall try that too,' said Tim reasonably. Then, realising that Lance was in no mood to co-operate, changed tack. 'But Lance, you're the only person I really want to quote from the English side. People see you as a sort of spokesman for the community. Plus, of course, you're a name that people know. And, you're easily the most articulate on the whole question,' he added for good measure.

Lance sat up in bed. Now completely awake, though still with throbbing temples, he recognised flattery when he heard it, but thought it entirely justified. He would give Tim a quote – after all, it would come better from him that some of the other idiots around – but he'd ask for something in return too. The events of yesterday evening were fresh and sore in his memory and one thing he was determined to do was to get revenge.

'Give me ten minutes,' he told Tim, and you'll have your quote. But, not before you answer a question for me.'

'Sure', said Tim. 'What is it?'

'Remind me which school in England Judith Hay used to work for before coming to France'.

Tim hesitated. 'Why do you want to know?' he asked. He already felt uncomfortable with the fact that he had mentioned recognising Judith to Lance. The man was spiteful and Tim was sure he didn't want the information for any innocent purpose. On the other hand, it would be easy enough for Lance to find out if he really wanted to by looking up the story on the internet.

'Just tell me,' said Lance. 'Or no quote.' Tim told him. What difference did it make, he reasoned.

As soon as he had telephoned Tim back with a quote to the

effect that the efforts of a few misguided Frenchmen were not going to drive the British community out of a country that they had every right to be in, Lance turned on his laptop. Right now, he wasn't so interested in punishing the French as he was the two English people who had incurred his wrath at the meeting.

Bill Bailey, he had dealt with nicely in the quote he had given to Tim by saying in what was supposed to be a rueful afterthought, that although the actions of the French were deplorable, he could understand their attitude in respect of the few uneducated arrivistes from Britain who spoiled everything for their fellow countrymen by refusing to integrate in any way and behaved like louts. He stopped short of naming Bailey but gave an example of 'a Northern, nouveau-riche loud-mouth who had arrived recently in their midst, purchased the biggest house around and proceeded to alienate everybody he encountered, both local and expatriate'. People like that, he explained, with no breeding, were an absolute menace and everybody would be a lot happier if he went back to the pit-town he came from.

Tim had chuckled when Lance had told him that. 'He gave you a bit of a drubbing last night, didn't he?' he said. 'What he said was an outrageous slander,' retorted Lance. 'It's class war as far as he's concerned. That's what it's about. The French won't run us out of town, but I sure as hell will try to run him out.'

Now, however, he turned his attention to the real menace in town – Miss Judith Hay, lately sacked from her

English public school. 'The Chase' he typed into the Google search engine. The name 'Judith Hay' alone hadn't yielded the story he was looking for. Immediately, a wealth of material about examination results, hockey tournaments and bursaries filled the screen. But, there at last was the entry of interest to him: 'The Chase – Resignation of Deputy Head – *The London Evening News* report June 5th.' Double-clicking on it, the story that the newspaper had carried that day came up in full.

Smiling to himself, in spite of the still throbbing temples, Lance read it through twice and pressed the print button. A few miles away, Judith, similarly cursed with a headache brought on by the anxiety she felt over Jean would have felt even worse had she heard Lance's printer whirring into action and realised its significance.

31

That Sunday, Tim's story about the meeting at Vevey and the anti-British activities was the lead story in the weekend supplement and had been followed up in their later editions by one or two of the Sunday tabloids delighted for another opportunity to indulge in the national sport of bashing the Frogs for their perceived insolence. Whilst these latter had fun with new versions of racist headlines like 'Up Yours Delors!', the *Sunday Times* piece was much more measured, and various contributors besides Tim had written 'think pieces' about the British migration to France and its implications.

The reaction in Vevey was mixed where every ruinously expensive copy of the *Sunday Times* (now available the same day thanks to a print-run in Marseilles) was sold out before 10 am. The Huffers and Puffers like Sue the tennis coach and her cronies were outraged that they and their ilk were now lambasted for their own failures in the integration process. 'A lot of the new migrants to rural France,' wrote one perceptive lady journalist who had spent time in France herself, 'get it wrong by doing the very same things for which they are quick to criticise immigrants to Britain… the number of people who think they can get by without learning French is amazing. They can't read road signs, appliance instructions or their own mortgage offers – and some of them have been in the country for decades. They rely on partners or children to translate and live lives as isolated as that of an illiterate 70-year-old plucked from a village in Bengal and marooned in an East End tower block…. My finger speaks French, they will say, meaning that they merely point at things when they go shopping.'

Whilst those to whom these words clearly applied were stung and outraged and stormed that it was typical of the British media to betray them, others smiled in recognition of what was a real problem in their community, where one half tried to fit in with the French (after all, they were mostly there through choice unlike most immigrants), whilst the other half grimly clung to their fragile sense of nationality by organising cricket matches and cream teas and making it a point of honour not to understand the language. That their new neighbours should be insulted by this form of jingoism either didn't occur to them, or they didn't care.

Bill Bailey was ominously quiet. He must have recognised himself as central to the feature, thought Tim, but nobody heard a peep out of him. It was only when people started noticing removal lorries outside his 'starter chateau' that it sunk in that Bill had been good as his word and gone to try his fortune on the Costa del Sol. Bryony, meantime, had long since packed her bags and was living happily with an English plumber in the next village.

For the next few days Tim was alternately feted or reviled as he walked around Vevey. Pleased though he was with the big spread he had got in the paper and the money that it would earn him, he was now almost completely preoccupied with what he thought of as his 'wine scoop'.

Alan had introduced him to Philippe de Masson as promised, and the old man had been intrigued. Tonight, as soon as Tim knew that the coast was clear and Roland was safely in his bar, he was going to drive Alan and Philippe to see the wine stash in the hills. In the meantime, he had done a lot of research in the local library and had read up about way that wine had become a valued commodity during the war in occupied France and was fought over more fiercely by the French and Germans than almost anything else.

More importantly, he had befriended a super-efficient librarian, a middle-aged scholar called Virginie, who knew all about the period he was interested in and was a keen local historian. She had provided him with a wealth of information about local conditions during the war, Resistance movements and which wine estates had suffered from German pillaging. Tim was sorely tempted to tell her what he had found but decided it should at least wait until Alan and Philippe had been to look. However, it occurred to him to ask Virginie if she knew anything about the incident in which Jean-Baptiste Chabot had been the only survivor in a Resistance train heist.

'Only what the locals say about it,' replied Virginie.

'Although, I think there is some documentation… I seem to recall that there is the station master's logbook which gives some details of what happened near St Pons, near here on the Beziers line. I know it was in 1940 – I'll try to lay my hands on it for you. I think I can get it from the main library in Montpellier.'

Virginie was as good as her word. Tim read the Henri Brillant's logbook with increasing excitement. At first, Brillant detailed every small bureaucratic headache that he had to put up with: his salary was always late; his staff were unreliable; various packages kept going missing. But one day in June 1940 something catastrophic happened. He heard the news when he came into work that morning. A train had derailed in his section because a switch had been thrown the wrong way, and now the entire contents of that train were missing – the best wines of the region, crates and crates of it, destined for Germany. Brillant was terrified his job would be on the line. To the authorities he claimed he knew nothing about what could have happened.

If that were so, Virginie told Tim, he would be the only one who didn't. She fetched him a couple of books to look at by French war historians who affirmed that all along the railroad lines of France at that time, railway workers, farmers and winegrowers were systematically stripping railway cars full of goods bound for Germany. 'It was almost a sport', said one. 'Our favourite amusement was cheating the Germans.'

Sometimes the trains were derailed and the contents

were ferried off to be hidden; sometimes people armed with jerry cans and rubber hoses would go to stations where barrels of wine were being loaded. When the guards were looking the other way (or were paid off), they would siphon all the wine out of the barrels which would then arrive empty, or full of water, at their destination, to the fury of the Germans. In this way, enormous quantities of wine was hidden from the Germans.

Defying the Germans was widespread but it was also dangerous. Tim read of plenty of incidents where the Germans were tipped off about a future wine raid for example, sometimes by French collaborators, and the result would be that the participants would be shot. This was what appeared to have happened on the night Jean-Baptiste and his local Resistance group went to derail a wine train near St Pons. Someone had tipped off the authorities and Jean-Baptiste was the only one to have survived. 'What happened to all the wine that night?' Tim asked Virginie. 'No-one knows,' she said. 'I assume if the Germans swooped before they had time to hide it, it would have ended up, as intended, in Germany.

Or in a cave in the *garrigue*, thought Tim, beside himself with excitement. Already, he could see the headlines. It could just be the same batch of wine. It's too much of a coincidence that the wine is hidden near where the derailing took place. His heart thumping, he thanked Virginie for her help and walked out into the heat of the early evening. It was only when he got to his car that he realised the huge significance of what he thought he had discovered.

If Roland, who was Jean-Baptiste's son, knew where the wine was then it stood to reason that Jean-Baptiste had told him. In fact, Jean-Baptiste must have hidden it there after the Germans shot his friends. Which could only mean one thing – that Jean-Baptiste, far from being a Resistance hero, was the one who had tipped off the authorities about the raid. And there was usually only one reason for such betrayal – money. Supposing – and this was something he had read about – supposing Jean-Baptiste was paid with fine wine rather than money – with some of the wine that was destined for Germany. It would make sense. He couldn't have hidden it in his own cellars; he couldn't have risked hiding it in anyone else's either. He had to hide it in the *garrigue* where he could access it in secret and sell it off little by little. And now his son was doing the same thing. My God, it was breathtaking. It just could have been like that, but how to prove it? He had to find out from which estates the wine had come that night and see if it matched the cases in the hideout. With luck, Alan's friend, the grand old *vigneron* Philippe, would have more information. He counted the hours until they were due to meet.

32

Once she was safely on the plane back to London, a weight seemed to lift from Jean's shoulders. She'd done it! She'd made the break with Lance. It made her feel positively light-headed. Why hadn't she done this years ago? It was so obvious now. It wasn't as though she couldn't afford it financially. Jean's parents were now very elderly and had downsized from a large house to a cottage in Sussex. The bulk of the considerable profit they made, they had put into a savings account for their daughter. Lance had known nothing of it and they had insisted that Jean keep it from him. 'You never know when you'll need it, darling,' her mother had said ominously when Jean had protested. Of course, Jean thought now, they'd been right all along; they'd seen this day coming. Her mother, in particular, had never taken to Lance, and with good reason it seemed. She herself had been blinded by all the attention at first and then Sarah had come along and it hadn't occurred to her to leave Lance then even though by the time Sarah was five, he had long since fallen out of love with her – and she with him. Perhaps that's why he had always given Sarah a hard time – perhaps it was nothing to do with his own perverted lust.

Well, whichever it was, she was damn well going to find out.

When Sarah had disappeared, she'd been so confused and miserable that it had seemed easier to go along with Lance's French plans and try to build a new life in different country. But once in France, puffed up by his new found status as a writer, Lance became even more impossible – and she more cowered than ever. But now, with all that she had learned lately, she had found new resolve. Of course, the first priority was to find Sarah and to make sure she was safe and well; once she had done that, she would make arrangements to come back to England and live on her own. She still had a small circle of friends in London with whom she could resume contact and in the meantime she could stay in the small flat that her parents had kept on in Kensington for when they came up to town to go to the theatre or the dentist. She would call them as soon as she arrived.

The pilot interrupted her chain of thought to announce their descent. Once they were through the cloud, Jean could see that the sky was a familiar murky grey and small drops of rain lashed against the windows. Hooray, she thought firmly, I'm home.

At about the time Jean landed in the drizzle at Stansted, Lance sat hunched at his computer sweating into his towelling robe cursing the sun. Wherever he moved it to, the screen always had a shaft a light on it, obscuring the text. Damn bloody Jean, he thought. She never fixed the blinds in this office properly. A large fly buzzed around the rim of his coffee cup before falling in. Lance resisted the urge to hurl the mug against the wall; if Jean had been here, he'd have hurled it at her.

Finally he retrieved the document he wanted and printed off several copies. Then he started to compose a letter to Gerald Thornton. When that was done, he attached one of the copies of the document and folded them both into an envelope. He would post it this afternoon. Leaning back in his chair, he felt a stab of satisfaction. That would shaft any romantic plans that Miss Judith Hay might be harbouring, he thought.

Once in her parents' small mansion flat off Kensington High Street, Jean's first and immediate need was to sleep. When she awoke, unsure where she was late in the afternoon, she decided to start her research. Clearly, Sarah's old friend Louise was the first point of contact. Naturally, she had consulted Louise when Sarah first ran away, but at that time Sarah was moving around between squats and not keeping anybody informed as to her whereabouts or her intentions. Four years had passed since then and Jean reckoned there was just an outside chance that Sarah had settled somewhere and rekindled her childhood friendship with Louise. She hadn't been especially friendly with Louise's parents but the girls had been in the same form at school and she vaguely remembered dropping Sarah off occasionally at a house in Chiswick – or was it Barnes? Surely, if they were still in London, they would be in the phone book.

Mathieson had an irritating number of entries but Jean narrowed it down to three likely ones, all of whom lived in west London. The second number she tried yielded a result of sorts. The woman who answered told her that she was renting the Mathiesons' house whilst they were in the Far East. John Mathieson was evidently a banker who was doing a stint in Singapore. She had a forwarding address for them, but no number, and no, sorry, she didn't know if they had a daughter or not.

Deflated but not defeated, Jean made herself a cup of tea and tried to think of other avenues to explore. Maddeningly, she had lost touch with other parents of Sarah's old friends. On the other hand, there was always the school… quickly she reached once again for the telephone directory.

The school office acknowledged that both Sarah and Louise were past pupils but had no present knowledge of them. The Old Girls' Society would only be able to help only if the girls themselves had kept in touch. A quick phone call later confirmed that they had not. However, the school secretary, possibly egged on to helpfulness by the note of desperation she detected in Jean's voice, suggested that she should try the internet. Jean's heart sank. Like most middle-aged women who didn't work and saw no need to keep in constant communication with friends by email, Jean's knowledge of the internet was limited.

'What should I look up?' she asked. 'Try 'Facebook' was the response. 'If you don't have an internet connection yourself, go to an internet café and ask someone there to help you.'

It was a start, Jean thought. It was probably too late to do anything useful now but tomorrow she would go and find one of these café things and try what the woman had suggested. She knew full well that Sarah would not have bothered with anything like 'Friends Reunited' but it was just possible that Lousie had. She would not give up. A girl of 24 cannot just disappear, however much she'd like to. Somebody would know where she was, but who was somebody, and how was Jean to find him or her?

Crying softly now, she cursed herself for giving up before, for losing precious time, for numbly following Lance to France like some dumb donkey and just letting go of her daughter. What a fool she had been! She blew her nose violently and wiped her eyes. Well, she deserved to suffer like this. God only knows what Sarah had been through. This time, she was not going to give up. She would place adverts in papers, she would stand in the street with a placard, she would badger the police until they let her make a television appeal. Oh, there was nothing she wouldn't do now.

33

Usually, Wuthering Heights was closed on a Monday since it was open all day Saturday but this particular Monday Gerald had set aside for his least favourite task – stock-taking, a dreary business if you're doing well, but a totally dismal one if not.

It was only 9am but already the heat was fierce. At least the relative cool of his office tucked away in an alcove in the basement would offer some respite. But as he turned the corner into his alleyway, his heart sank still further. The local graffiti artiste had been busy it seemed, and the wooden door of the shop was once again sprayed with unintelligible obscenities in silver paint. Gerald had only scrubbed it the week before and the thought of repeating the routine so soon in the heat made him want to weep. Fucking little shit, he thought furiously. You'd think he'd give it a break on a Sunday. If only I could get hold of him I'd hammer him to death – or Ged would. Really, there were days now – plenty of days – when he thought he'd pack it all up and creep back to Britain with his tail between his legs.

Moving to France had served its purpose for him these

last ten years. He'd done his mourning for his wife here and the pain had finally receded. He'd realised his long-held ambition of running a bookshop (and found that most of the time it was just as mundane and as much hard work as selling anything – harder, in fact, since books were a commodity many people could do without) and he'd made a life of sorts for himself out here and learned to love many aspects of it. He was, however, he now acknowledged to himself, still rather lonely. He had made one or two good friends through the bookshop and had a couple of desultory affairs which had fizzled out, but that was the extent of it.

Perhaps it was time to call it a day… on the other hand, he had to admit, now that he came to think of it, that just lately he'd been feeling more positive about life. He was too much of an old hand at analysing his own feelings not to know that this new source of contentment was linked with his unsought and unexpected friendship with Judith Hay. They hadn't seen much of each other but already he felt naturally at ease with her. At first she interested him because of her quick intelligence and lack of pretension or social airs. Now, he realised, he had begun to be physically attracted to her as well. She was not conventionally beautiful but she had a sort of nervous grace about her that was very appealing. He also actually liked the fact that she was so buttoned up and unforthcoming about herself. It would be a challenge, he felt, to tease some details of her life out of her. She was curiously reluctant to talk of her previous existence but he had the impression she had been badly hurt – perhaps that was why she was here in France.

She wouldn't be the first to think that you could offload your baggage just by moving away; sadly, most people took their baggage with them as they learned to their cost. He felt a sudden stab of protectiveness and affection for her. Well, he would see her soon – they had arranged to have dinner out midweek at a new restaurant in the old quarter. He was looking forward to it.

It wasn't until later in the day that Gerald bothered to pick up the post that was waiting for him. It had looked like the usual pile of bills but now, as he stopped work to make himself a cup of tea, he could see that there was a white envelope amongst the buff ones. Inside were two sheets of plain paper. On one, computer typed, he read: 'Thought you might like to know a little more about your girlfriend.' No signature. On the other was a computer printout of a newspaper story about a school in England. Before he read on, Gerald looked at the envelope. That too held no clues. His address had been typed and the stamp obliterated the postmark. Mystified he read on. When he had finished, he sat down heavily and put his head in his hands.

In August, the sun burns the *garrigue* to dusty straw and there is the ever-present threat of forest fires which rage each year across the south of France. When Tim had arrived in the Languedoc, despite the heat, the scrubland had been vibrant with broom and gorse and if you went walking early in the morning or at dusk, as he did most days, the mixed scents of herbs and pine were sharp and sweet. Now, as he and Alan and Philippe de Masson walked along the cart track, the overwhelming scent was of dry lavender with just the occasional whiff of fennel, anise or wild thyme carried on the hot wind.

Piggy, meantime, had other scents on her mind as she zig-zagged back and forwards tracking other animals by their territorial markers.

They had left the car half a mile away and the heat was getting to the old man. He stopped and mopped his brow with a silk handkerchief. 'Oof,' he remarked. 'This summer has been the worst. I fear we shall have a bad autumn too. Generally after such heat, we have dramatic storms which can flood the vineyards – and the villages too.' For a nano-second, Tim thought wistfully of England and the temperate climate there. Only this morning on the telephone his mother had complained that it was already quite chilly at night. When Tim told her that the temperature hadn't dropped much below 35 degrees in the south of France for over two months – and that it remained almost as hot at night – she sounded alarmed. 'Don't forget to put on lots of sun cream,' she reminded him. 'Even here, it says on the news you should put it on if you're out much during the day. Freya knows someone who got skin cancer after a holiday in Cornwall.' Tim had to smile. Sunscreen and hats in summer; haliborange and vests in winter; for his mother he would remain ossified at about twelve years old.

Now, sunscreen was the last thing on his mind. Like a terrier sighting a rat he was, he felt, within sight of his quarry and as nervous as hell. If his theory about Roland was right then he was on to a really big story. A journalist first and foremost, he hadn't got as far as thinking about the possible consequences for the community.

They rounded a corner giving splendid views over the valley and forked off down an even smaller track which led to the cave. Piggy forged ahead, knowing where they were headed, followed by Tim and Philippe now leaning heavily on Alan's arm. Tim hoped the old man wasn't going to expire just as they got there. He bent down and cleared the entrance to the cave and the three of them squeezed in. Once inside, it opened out and when their eyes grew accustomed to the gloom, they could make out dozens of cases of wine, some covered in dirt and cobwebs, some recently opened up. Alan whistled: 'My God' he breathed.

Philippe bent down with difficulty to examine some of the bottles. Tim handed him a powerful torch so that he could read the labels. He looked at bottles from several cases before commenting – an agonising amount of time for Tim, who was pacing round the cave unable to stand the tension. At last he straightened up. 'You were right, my friend,' he said to Tim. 'This is stolen wine from several great wine estates – and not just from round here. Some of it is exceptional Bordeaux.'

'So what do you think happened?' asked Tim, unable to contain himself.

'I know what happened', said Philippe. 'Let us go outside into the air and we can discuss it.'

They stumbled out, blinking in the sunshine and Tim found a flattish rock for Philippe to sit on. He sat slowly, and once again wiped his brow. Alarmingly, he looked as though he might cry. 'This is a serious find,' he began. Undoubtedly, this is German loot. They stole huge quantities from all the very best wine estates. Most of it got back to Germany but there was much resistance activity round here too and sometimes the wine was hijacked on its journey by train or lorry, and returned to the estates. Many people died in the attempt. Sometimes, there would be a traitor who knew of the hijacking plans and often they were paid for their services with wine. After the war, we mostly knew who those people were. Some disappeared, some thrived. It was a bad part of France's history and most people do not like to talk about it, even now. This man, Roland, who you have told me about – perhaps he too was paid with wine. Tell me what you know of him. Is he an old man?

'No,' chipped in Alan. 'He's only about my age. He must have been born after the war.'

'Yes,' said Tim excitedly. 'But, it was his father – Jean-Baptiste who was involved. I've done all the research on it.'

'You had better tell us what you know', said Philippe.

Tim told them the story about Jean-Baptiste and the derailed train. Philippe nodded his head. 'Now I remember something of this', he said gravely. 'Perhaps Jean-Baptiste was not the resistance hero he claims to be. And now, his son, Roland, is living off the profits of his treachery. It is possible, I'm afraid.'

'But what are we going to do about it?' asked Alan. 'It's an extremely difficult situation – and so long after the war too.'

Tim hadn't really thought about anything except the banner headlines. It was then that they heard a shot.

34

It was impossible to sleep. Finally Judith gave up and padded upstairs to her terrace. Even the tiles were warm beneath her feet but at least out here there was a faint breeze stirring. She lay on her swing seat from where she could see the village clock tower illuminated. It was 2.40 am. In the distance she could hear a dog barking but for once her noisy Spanish neighbours had shut up early and moved all their chairs from the pavement inside. Sometimes they were still shouting the odds at each other at this time outside, their voices rising indignantly as if in argument, then breaking out in shrill laughter. God knows what they found to talk about night after night. There was a group of six or seven of them, sometimes with small children who ran around shrieking. One of the men had lost his voice – perhaps to cancer – and spoke in what she assumed was a machine-generated growl. When she had first heard it, it had given her a start – he sounded like a fictional serial killer about to strike. The voice was produced with evident effort and yet he seemed to be the dominant one in the group – the one the others deferred to, the one who appeared to have the last word. And often he had a small child on his knee so they clearly didn't think him a monster on account of it.

Tonight she might have welcomed their ceaseless chatter. In the silence she had more time to concentrate on her own thoughts and these span round in her head uselessly. What to do, what to do. Oh Christ. She wished she didn't know anything about Lance.

Jean's latest visit and revelations had filled her with apprehension. And she hadn't been able to get hold of her since then either. For three days she had telephoned at intervals, making sure she dialled a number first so that she could put the phone down if Lance answered and he wouldn't be able to trace the call. Twice this had happened; the rest of the calls were intercepted by a message machine. Several times she had driven past the house to see if she could see her, but there was no sign of her. Sometimes Lance's car was there, but never hers. She must have gone away for a while. Or else, Lance had murdered her. At this time of night, that seemed a distinct possibility.

She had tried calling Gerald to talk it over with him – the one person she felt she could trust, but he had sounded strange and offhand on the phone and told her he couldn't talk to her right then. 'Shall I still see you on Thursday night?' she asked anxiously. There had been an ominous pause. 'Yes, I suppose so,' he said leadenly. 'Come here as planned at 7.00pm'. Judith had replaced the phone feeling sick wondering what the matter with him was. She was more shattered than she liked to think.

Gerald was beginning to mean a lot to her and it was intolerable to think of their friendship ending when it had hardly begun. What on earth could she have done to make him sound so… not unpleasant exactly, but unhappy – and cold with her. With a slight pang, she wondered if he had a woman with him – a lover perhaps. After all, why shouldn't he? She realised she knew very little about his life but somehow she had got the impression that he didn't have anybody around – and also, and here maybe she was getting her wires crossed – that he liked seeing her. All at once she felt desperately sad. But, then, she reasoned, perhaps it's nothing like that, perhaps something's gone wrong at the shop. It was going to be very difficult waiting until Thursday to find out, but she knew she mustn't call again before then.

After a while, she crept downstairs again and fell into a deep sleep in which one nightmare pursued the next. She woke up late feeling groggy and had to drink a couple of strong coffees to galvanise her into action. Damn, it was already 11.00 am and she had to go to the supermarket to get some provisions – irritatingly in this part of France they too closed down for lunch at 12.30 and you had to wait until the middle of the afternoon to get anything done. She simply couldn't face another meal of tinned tuna or boiled egg so she must get going. Distractedly, she glanced at her message machine as she unlocked the door – it was blinking. Hell, she must have slept right through the telephone ringing. Pressing play, hoping it was Gerald, she held her breath as she heard Jean's voice telling her that she was in London in case she was worried. 'I'm here to find Sarah,' she said. 'Talking with you has finally clinched it. I'm going to do the right thing now. Thank you, Judith, for listening – and… I'm sorry to involve you in all this. I'll call again.'

Judith let out a sigh of relief. Thank God she was OK. That perhaps was one less thing to worry about. But meantime, Lance was still at large. She wondered whether he knew that Jean had gone.

Fifteen minutes later, she was in Intermarché hurriedly dumping fresh fruit, bread and salad in her trolley when she caught sight of Camilla Stanhope at the fish counter. Her first instinct was to wheel the trolley round and leave but at that moment Camilla saw her too and waved. 'Hi', she said. 'How are you? We only got down here yesterday.' They exchanged news and pleasantries for a few minutes then Judith plucked up the courage to ask after Sophie. 'Oh, we couldn't get her to come with us this time,' she said. 'For some reason she absolutely refused. Said she wanted just to chill out at home and see friends. Usually she loves it out here and can't wait to work on her tan. Such a nuisance because we're going to stay with friends next week who are giving a teenage party that she's invited to, but still, it's quite relaxing for me and Rex not to have any of the children around.'

Well, this was her cue, thought Judith. It's now or never. 'Do you think her not wanting to come has anything to do with Lance?'

'Lance?' Camilla smiled in a puzzled way. 'Why ever should it?'

So, Sophie hadn't said anything. 'It's just… it's just that I heard something worrying about him,' mumbled Judith. 'Something about him preferring young girls and trying it on with Sophie.' There, it was out. But Camilla laughed. 'Oh nonsense,' she said. 'Sophie adores Lance. He's like an uncle to her.'

'I think it's more than that,' Judith managed to say. 'I think Sophie may have been… hurt… by him.' Camilla's smile faded. 'I'm not sure I know what you're trying to say Judith, 'but I think I would know if my own daughter was hurt.' Then seeing Judith's abject expression, she changed tack. 'Look, maybe there's been a misunderstanding but Rex and I have known Lance for years and so has Sophie. What's bugging Sophie at the moment is school. She got a really bad report for the first time this term and she's sulking. Apart from that, she's fine. Anyway, I must go – we've got the Knights coming for lunch.' She started walking away saying over her shoulder, 'see you at the next barbeque no doubt!'

Judith pushed her trolley away blinking back angry tears. What a cow Camilla was – she just didn't want to know. Or worse, she did know, but she wasn't going to do anything about it. Poor Sophie. She probably knew that she wouldn't be believed if she did tell her parents. And anyway, it was too late to do anything about it now. People like that didn't deserve children, but her attitude wasn't uncommon. Judith had seen several parents like that at The Chase – more anxious about their next dinner party than the welfare of their children. As for her, she would butt out now. There was absolutely nothing further to be done. In future, she'd try to keep out of other people's business. It wasn't as if she had wanted to know it in the first place. Even Jean had to fight her own battles from now on.

35

At nine am sharp Jean was outside the internet café in Kensington High Street waiting for it to open. Once inside, the young man behind the counter was helpful. He typed in the website Jean had written on a scrap of paper and waited with her whilst Friends Reunited came up. 'Now you just follow the instructions till you find the person you're looking for,' he said cheerfully, thinking that it was a strange request for a woman of her age. Surely her school must have closed down years ago.

Immediately, a quotation on the site caught her eye: 'Thanks to Friends Reunited, I have found my son who I have not seen since he was 13 and I have discovered that I am a grandfather!' This accompanied a photograph of a smiling old man with his arm round a younger man holding a child by the hand. Jean's heart beat faster. That could be her soon! Surely it was an omen. She was so nervous that she found it hard to type although she had been trained as a secretary. Gingerly finding her way round the keyboard, she typed in the name of Sarah's old London day school and tried to remember which year she wanted. Must have been 1984 that Sarah left. A list of about fifteen names came up. Some she recognised immediately – she'd got the right year group then. Heart hammering, she looked down the list, first for Sarah. Please god, she thought, please. No Sarah. But there, in the middle amongst the other M's was Louise Mathieson. Yes!

'I've found the name!' she called to the young man. 'Now what do I do please?' He came over and showed her how to double click on the name. A page of information came up. 'OK now?' he said. She seemed mightily excited just to have found the name of some old school friend he thought.

Jean scanned the information. 'Louise Mathieson (84) went to sixth form college and then to University College, London to read medicine', she read. She is now a practising GP in Oxford where she lives with her husband Sean McCauley who teaches at the university. She would love to see any old school friends who are passing through Oxford.'

There was an opportunity to email Louise but it meant registering on the site and in any case Jean didn't have a computer or an email address herself. But it didn't matter. Lousie was a GP in Oxford – she could easily find out her surgery number by looking up an Oxford telephone directory in the library. Her spirits higher than they had been for ages, Jean paid the young man and stepped out into the brightening day. Now for the library.

Within two hours, Jean was on a train from Paddington to Oxford. She had found and phoned the number of

Louise's surgery but Louise wasn't there. The receptionist said that she would be taking surgery that afternoon between 2pm and 4pm. Jean reckoned she would be in Oxford by 1 pm and that the simplest thing would be to go and speak directly to Louise. She could perhaps waylay her before or after the surgery. Of course, it may be that Louise couldn't tell her anything about Sarah, but there again, maybe she could. They had been inseparable as children, and this time Jean was determined to leave nothing to chance.

Oxford had changed beyond all recognition. Jean had been there frequently as a young woman to stay with cousins. And once, shortly after she had met him, Lance had taken her to a May Ball at St John's College. It was probably the most romantic evening they had ever spent together. The weather was perfect, she recalled. A golden evening. Marquees on college lawns, live bands, beautiful sophisticated people of whom Jean had been very shy, in evening dress, and later a punt on the river as dawn broke. Throughout their marriage Jean had clung to the memory trying to revive all the feelings she had then.

Oxford Station itself was the first surprise when Jean alighted from her train. It all looked modern. And then, across from the station itself was a building she'd never seen before with a sort of green ziggurat on top of it. Passing by the glass entrance she peered at the sign: The Wafik Said School of Business. She sighed. Well, what did she expect? John Betjeman to come cycling round the corner composing Summoned By Bells?

North Oxford, however, where Louise's surgery was to be found, looked gratifying unchanged. The wide leafy roads flanked by huge Victorian houses which had been built for the University Dons and their families as soon as they were allowed to marry, made her nostalgic for the happy summer holidays she had passed playing with her cousins in the orchard behind a house similar to these off the Woodstock Road.

Louise's surgery was in a road closer to the Banbury Road and the bustling little shopping area known as Summertown. Many of the little shops she remembered were still there but Marks & Spencer had opened up in the high street – a food store only catering for the large numbers of wealthy residents who she knew had flocked into that part of Oxford in recent years, anxious for their offspring to attend prestigious prep schools nearby. The Dons themselves of course could just about run to takeaway M & S sandwiches for lunch, whilst endless astonishingly scruffy looking students filled all the outside café and pub chairs, some even sprawling on the pavement with their bottles of lager – even the girls. How times had changed, she thought wistfully. She remembered coming shopping here with her aunt when it was all very sedate and everyone wore hats.

She turned into Louise's road and found the surgery, a small modern building at the corner of a residential road. It was just before two. The receptionist asked her if she could come back to see Louise at 4pm when surgery ended as Dr Mathieson had non-stop appointments. She promised she would tell her it was urgent. It was what Jean had expected. As she turned to leave, she saw a young woman getting out of her car in the small car park at the side. Slim, business-like, neatly dressed with shoulder-length blonde hair in a neat bob, carrying a briefcase. Ah, that would be Louise. She looked at her fleetingly not wishing to embarrass her; little did she know that Louise's future happiness depended on her.

Louise was waiting for in her office when she returned just after four. 'Mrs Campion', she exclaimed, when she saw Jean. 'It is you… I wasn't sure. Shirley said that a Mrs Campion wanted to see me but I thought it was so unlikely… how very nice to see you after all this time.'

'Jean… please call me Jean. Oh Louise, my dear, you're so grown up now – and a doctor! Thank you so much for seeing me. I wouldn't have come like this but…', she faltered, tears involuntarily springing to her eyes, 'I'm desperate, Louise.'

'Sit down, Jean', said Louise gently, seeing how upset she was. 'How can I help?'

'It's about Sarah,' sniffed Jean. 'You know she left home at sixteen and then we lost touch? I looked everywhere for her… you remember?

'Yes, of course I do,' said Louise. 'I lost touch with her too. She was going through a bad time and I think she just wanted to cut loose from everything and everybody that she knew. I was cut up about it because we were so close but by then I was at college and life just took over I suppose. Do you see her now?'

'No', cried Jean. 'That's just the point. I still have no idea where she is or what has become of her and… it was important then, but it's even more important now. I think I know why she left home like that. Oh Louise, do you know how I can find her again? Has she contacted you at all over the years?'

'I had a card from her just over a year ago,' said Louise. She sent it to my parents' house in Chiswick and it finally got forwarded to me. She said she was thinking of me because it was my birthday and she hoped I was all right. She sent me her new address in London and said if I was ever there, she'd like to see me again. I think I wrote it down… I'm afraid I never did go and see her. I'd just moved up here and got married and started in this practice and… well, I should have made time for her. She said she was OK again but had been having a difficult time. I got the impression she'd been in a clinic for a while for drug addiction. Oh, Jean, I'm so sorry…', she put her arm around Jean's shaking shoulders. I didn't realise you still didn't know where she was.'

'We've been in France,' Jean sobbed. 'She may even have tried to get in contact again. Poor, poor Sarah. I feel so terrible about her. I tried to forget about her, you know, and start a new life. She just about broke my heart. But I couldn't… forget about her I mean. And now, I must find her, Louise. Please try to find that address for me – she may still be there. Oh God, I hope she is.'

'Of course I will. It'll be at home in my address book if it's anywhere. Look, Jean, come home with me now and I'll try to find it and we can talk more comfortably there.'

Nursing a cup of tea whilst Louise rummaged upstairs at her house in Headington, Jean tried to breathe normally. She felt sick and giddy and her heart was thumping uncomfortably against her ribs. If Louise couldn't find the address, then what? She imagined herself once again pacing the streets peering into every young woman's face she met. She jerked her head up as Louise came back in the room. 'Got it!' she said excitedly. 'I knew I'd kept it somewhere just in case….'

Jean fumbled for her glasses to read the address on the bit of paper Louise gave her. Her eyes swam. Wimbledon, she made out. Flat 2, Beechcroft Road, Wimbledon, London SW17. 'Was there a telephone number?' she asked. 'No, said Louise. I think that was one reason I never got in touch – it was too difficult. Perhaps she doesn't have a telephone. Or just uses a mobile nowadays.'

'Well, that's an enormous help, anyway, Louise,' said Jean, impulsively giving the girl a hug. You've been so kind – I really can't thank you enough. I shall go to this address tomorrow and see if she's still there.'

'I really hope she is,' replied Louise. 'And please let me know if you find her. I would like to see her again, very much. But…', she hesitated, 'What did you mean when you said you knew now why she had left home? Is it what I think it is?'

Jean looked at her. Then she opened her handbag and drew out the old photograph she had found in Lance's desk. 'Do you remember this?' she asked, handing it to Louise.

Louise frowned. 'Sarah and I topless on a beach', she said slowly. 'Yes, I think I do. We were in Cornwall with you and your husband. He took lots of pictures of us.'

'Yes,' said Jean heavily. 'I thought so. I found this recently in Lance's desk and I wondered why he had kept it. I couldn't remember taking any pictures.

I… I've since learnt things about Lance… things I would prefer not to know. How he likes young girls… how…', her voice faltered.

Louise interrupted. 'I never wanted you to know', she said brokenly. 'I thought you might suspect, but you didn't, did you? Not until it was too late….'

Jean felt all the colour drain from her face. 'Did he… did he interfere with you, Louise? You can tell me now, she added as she saw the girl's eyes fill with tears.

'Yes, he did. He tried to rape me, Jean. It was at the end of that holiday when you and Sarah had gone off shopping or something. He got me on my own and tried to force himself on me. He was like a wild animal, violent, not himself… I was terrified.'

'Oh my god', said Jean. 'What did you do? Oh, Louise, I'm so sorry.'

'I screamed and I bit him. He only laid off when we heard your car coming back to the house. I ran off and hid. Sarah came looking for me and I told her. We were only fifteen.'

'What did Sarah say?' asked Jean, knowing that the answer would change everything.

'She said he did it to her all the time. That you mustn't know about it. That I must never tell.'

36

They all froze as the shot rang in their ears. 'Quick, back into the cave', hissed Alan. He helped the old man back in and Tim followed. They stood looking at each other in the gloom, the seriousness of the situation beginning to sink in. They had stumbled across a crime scene; worse, a festering secret that had been well kept over the years and that threatened to expose its perpetrators as war criminals. Suddenly, for Tim, the excitement of the journalistic quarry was over. This was life and death, not some game of amateur sleuth. 'Roland must have followed us,' he whispered. 'I'm sorry. It was crazy to have come out here like this. We should have told the police in the first place.' He found he was shaking. Alan too looked terrified. 'What the hell is the best thing to do now?' he asked no-one in particular.

Only Philippe seemed calm. 'If it is Roland, we must confront him', he said. 'But we'll get shot,' hissed Tim. 'I don't think so,' said Philippe. 'But in any case we cannot stay here. I will go outside and see.'

'No! Don't be stupid!' Alan clutched at his arm but Philippe shook him off. 'I'm an old man,' he said lightly. 'It doesn't matter what happens to me, and if he is there, I'm the only one who can talk to him.' He bent down painfully and walked slowly out into the light.

Several heart-stopping moments went passed while Tim and Alan waited, straining to hear what was going on. Silence. 'Come on,' said Tim finally. 'I can't stand this; we can't just stay here.' They scrambled out after Philippe who was standing a little further on lighting a cigarette. He turned when he saw them. 'There is nobody here', he said. Of course, the shot sounded at a distance so it may take some time.'

'Could it be hunters?' Tim asked hopefully. 'In August?' said Alan. 'I don't think so; they only start to hunt in October.' On the other hand it could just have been some idiot out killing rabbits.

Gingerly, they picked their way through the brambles that partly obscured the cave and came out onto the track. There was a sudden rustling in the bushes nearby and a yelping. 'Piggy!' Cried Tim. 'I'd forgotten about you. Where are you?' He followed the small whining sounds and found the dog, frightened and panting in the undergrowth. 'Oh my God, she's bleeding,' he cried. 'He got her, the bastard.' Piggy had a flesh wound in her side where a flap of skin was loose. Tim took out a handkerchief and pressed to her side to stem the blood. 'Quickly, Alan, help me get her to the car.'

At that moment, Philippe looked up. In the distance he could make out three young boys scrambling to climb up higher out of sight. 'Ah,' he said, 'I think those are our culprits. Some boys with an air rifle; they thought it would be fun to take aim at the dog no doubt.'

'Little bastards!' breathed Tim. 'I'd go after them if I could but we must get Piggy to the vet.'

'Well, thank god it's not Roland,' said Alan, 'or it wouldn't just be Piggy who was bleeding.'

Between them Alan and Tim carried Piggy to the car as gently as they could. It seemed to take forever because she was heavy and upset and Philippe couldn't go fast but eventually they lay Piggy in the back on a rug and headed for the vet in Vevey.

Later, back at Alan's house, the three of them discussed what they should do now. Piggy's wound had been superficial. The bullet must have grazed her but luckily hadn't entered her. She was more frightened than hurt but the vet was keeping her in overnight to be on the safe side.

It was decided that Philippe should notify the appropriate authorities and this he said he would do in the morning. 'There is nothing to be done this late,' he explained. 'Alan will take me home and you must leave it to me. I know people; I know what to do. The police will want to speak to you both later I'm sure and you, Tim, will have your story. Personally, I feel sad and ashamed. This will have terrible repercussions in the community; it will revive old memories and people will take it hard if it is proved that Jean-Baptiste was a collaborator who got paid off with this wine haul. Nobody likes to be reminded of the war.'

It was all a bit of an anti-climax, Tim thought as he drove home. Subdued by the old man's speech, and worried about his dog, he began to think it might have been better never to have found the wine stash. He could have got them all killed; he damn nearly did get Piggy killed. And he dreaded to think what was going to happen in the village. Although Roland and his father deserved to be punished, there were bound to be those who resented his – a foreigner's – interference if they got to hear about it. Where the war years were concerned, he had learnt at the library and from Virginie, it was sometimes better to leave well alone. Some people hadn't behaved well during the war, sure, but they were exceptional times. There were many people living around the area who were thought to have co-operated with the Germans in some way but who had been mostly forgiven afterwards. On the other hand, Jean-Baptiste, if his theory was correct, had deliberately caused the deaths of his friends – courageous young men who were doing their best to fight the enemy. He wasn't just slipping the Germans the best meat available like the surly butcher in La Prairie who was known to still think that the Germans should have won the war. Surely, he should be brought to justice.

Once at home, he flung himself down on his bed fully clothed, unable to think clearly and too shattered by the day's events to get undressed and now feeling unaccountably sad. He was no longer sure about the events he had set in motion.

The next morning he felt no better. Damn, this wasn't how it was supposed to be. The huge adrenalin rush he had got from discovering the wine and then following up the clues had all but disappeared now that the Philippe had identified the wine as being stolen during the war and was about to alert the authorities. What would happen, Tim wondered. Would Roland be publicly arrested and put on trial? Would Jean-Baptiste be dragged through the streets by a lynch mob? Would the English papers even be interested?

First of all, he must go to see how Piggy was and bring her home. A wave of affection broke over him. He loved that dog; it would have been horrendous if anything worse had happened to her just because he wouldn't mind his own business. Then, he thought, I'll go to see Fern, see if she can have lunch with me – if anybody can make me feel better, she can. But before he had time to leave the house, his telephone rang.

'It's Gerald', said the voice the other end. And then without any preliminaries, 'What do you know about Judith Hay?'

'What do you mean?' asked Tim in an unnaturally squeaky voice, playing for time. The man sounded bloody pissed off. He was Judith's great friend wasn't he?

'I know Judith, but not well', he said, she's a friend of Fern's. I like her.'

'If you like her,' said Gerald stonily, 'why have you betrayed her?'

'I don't know what you're talking about', lied Tim,

feeling cold and shaky.

'I think you do. I think in your capacity as a so-called journalist you have found something out about her past life in England and you have passed that information on to people who only wish Judith harm. Am I making myself clear?'

'Are you talking about her being sacked from the school she taught in?' Tim asked. He thought he knew what was coming. That fucking monster Lance must have started spreading the shit.

'Of course I am,' said Gerald. 'How would anyone here know if you hadn't told them? I've put two and two together and come up with your name. You're a journalist. You must have seen the story in the papers about her and talked about it. Somebody, who chooses to be anonymous naturally, has sent me a copy of a newspaper cutting detailing the events at her school. I don't suppose that's you but am I right in thinking you told Lance Campion?'

Tim gulped. Could this morning get any worse? He knew he had to come clean.

'Look Gerald, I don't wish Judith any harm at all. I happened to work on that story of her sacking when I was on the *Tribune*. In fact, oddly enough, it's the reason I got sacked myself, though that's another story. I thought nothing of it until I came out here and happened to recognise Judith from the pictures I'd seen and from the little I knew of her having been a teacher at a public school in England. Without thinking, I mentioned it to Lance whom I saw that evening in a bar just as a curious thing. I didn't know he would do anything with it. I didn't know he harboured any bad feelings towards Judith. Why should I? What's he got against her? If it is him who's sent you the cutting and I'm the cause of it, then I'm very sorry – I really am. I can see it's a rotten rumour to get about, but I really wasn't to know.

Something in Tim's voice made Gerald hold off from further recriminations. After all, he was just a harmless gossip; he couldn't have known what the story meant, either to Lance or for Gerald. No, the person who worked that one out was Lance. Who else would have sent him the cutting and the malicious note? Judith had been frightened of him with reason it seemed.

'Oh forget it,' he said wearily. 'Just don't do any more damage by talking about it to anyone else. Judith is entitled to a private life – we all are.' He hung up.

Tim replaced the receiver feeling wretched and sat down heavily on his bed, his head in his hands. Looked like he was creating trouble for everyone. Perhaps it was time to move on again.

31

Unaware of all this anguish on her behalf, Judith started to get ready for her evening out with Gerald. She was nervous because he had sounded so odd and strained – unfriendly even – on the phone. But since she couldn't think what might have caused it, she decided just to play it cool and not even ask him about it when she saw him.

She dressed carefully putting on a cream linen shift dress which flattered her slim figure and contrasted well with her brown arms and legs. The sea and sun had flatteringly streaked her dark blonde hair which she pinned back in a comb. She wore no make-up and no jewellery. She never had and it suited her that way. Everything about Judith was unadorned, unfussy, unobtrusive. Perhaps that was why some people didn't even really notice her. She didn't court attention and generally speaking she didn't get it either. Oh well, she thought, I can't change the way I am. Anxiously, she peered into the mirror and saw reflected back at her anxious green eyes in a tanned, oval face, with a dusting of freckles over her nose. She should have been pleased; she didn't look her age – unlike poor Jean who had aged about ten years in the past few months – but even so she felt sick with nerves.

As she left her house, she noticed that the anti-English slogan had been scrubbed off her wall. It looked as though the mayor had been good as his word and had sprung into action. She knew it hadn't been personal now, but even so it left a nasty taste in the mouth. She wondered about this business of living in someone else's country. Of course, people had always done it everywhere, sometimes successfully, sometimes not. Here in the south of France – not the fleshpots of the Côte d'Azur 'a sunny place for shady people' – but this real slice of southern France where the rate of immigration of more sophisticated Europeans was, she supposed, rather daunting for the people who had lived here for generations without much mobility.

The big cities such as Montpellier, Nimes, Beziers and Perpignan were used to immigrants from North Africa. Hence the popularity of M. Le Pen in the south. But here in the villages, time had stood almost still. La Prairie still had families in it who could trace their ancestors back to the 13th century. And many of her neighbours never went further afield than Vevey. It wasn't so surprising that there was some hostility. But by no means everywhere. Judith was still charmed by the small shopkeepers with their elaborate formal manners and their unfailing '*Bonjour Madame*' when she went anywhere, and '*Bonne Journée*' when she left. It would be a terrible pity if their way of life was eroded by the relatively uncouth incomers. How long was it since anyone had heard 'Good Morning Madam' from an English shopkeeper?

*

Judith parked her car in an underground car park near the Arc de Triomphe in Montpellier. It was a little further to walk to Gerald's shop from here but it was her favourite part of town. The Arch, which resembled its namesake in Paris stood at the entrance to the Promenade du Peyrou, a long promenade where open-air festivals were held in the days of Louis XIV. A statue of the Sun King himself stands in its centre looking towards the town. From Peyrou there was a lovely view over the town one way and over towards the blue Cevennes mountains in the distance.

Judith strolled down the Rue Foch, a stately street of 17th and 18th-century mansions, now home to smart designer shops that nobody ever seemed to go in, and then turned off into the network of small streets, picturesque squares and alleys that made up the medieval old town. Wuthering Heights was in a tiny stone-flagged street near the Place St-Ravy where one could make out the scant remains of the palace of the Kings of Majorca. Normally, she loved this quarter but tonight, her nerves plus the distinct smell of cat pee unsettled Judith and made her feel queasy.

When she went into the shop, it only got worse. Gerald was supposed to have closed but he was still talking to a customer. He barely acknowledged her so Judith was forced to feign interest in the shelves of books whilst she waited. Her eyes began to smart with tears but she managed to blink them back. What was wrong with him? His conversation with the customer dragged on and he was making little effort to end it. Finally, however, the man left with a package of books under his arm and Gerald turned to her. 'Shall we go and have a drink at the bar on the corner?' he said gruffly. 'I need to sit down and talk to you.' Judith felt suddenly angry and threw caution to the winds. 'Why, what have I done?' she asked. 'You make me feel like a naughty child hauled before the headmistress.'

'Huh', was Gerald's response. 'Funny you should say that… come on.'

With a sinking heart, Judith followed him out of the shop and waited while he locked up. They walked in silence the short distance to the bar.

Gerald ordered himself a beer and her a white wine without even asking her what she'd like. 'Look,' she said furiously, 'if the evening is going to continue like this, I think I'd better go home.'

'Yes, maybe you should,' said Gerald, 'but not before I show you what came for me in the post the other day.' He handed Judith two pieces of A4 paper. Shakily, she took them and started to read. The familiar newspaper story leapt out at her – she had no need to re-read that; the message on the other piece of paper made her gorge rise. 'How dare you!' she cried, standing up and scraping her chair back noisily. 'How dare you present me with these like this? I don't know who this is from, but I can guess. It's horrible but what's even worse is your attitude and behaviour. You want some explanation, is that it? You want to know if it's true? Well, judging from your demeanour, you've already judged me guilty. The trial is over. I don't owe you an explanation at all – you're supposed to be my friend. Why should you care anyway?' Trembling with anger, she slammed down her drink and ran out of the bar.

At that moment, Gerald realised he'd made what was probably the biggest mistake of his life. What the hell was he thinking of? Treating Judith like a criminal just because he was disappointed that she might prefer women to men.

Pushing back his chair so forcefully that it crashed to the ground, he sprinted after her into the street. He saw her turning a corner, now walking very fast but not running. In two seconds he caught up with her. 'Judith', he cried catching her round the waist. She spun round, her face streaming with tears. 'Oh Judith.' He hugged her clumsily. 'I'm so sorry, so very sorry. How can you forgive me? I've been a fool, a boorish fool. I was just so cut up when I got that… so unhappy… so worried about you. It doesn't matter what you are or who you are or anything about your past. I care about you very much. I *am* your friend, whatever you think. I admit it, it came as a blow to read about you. I thought….'

'You thought we might become more than friends?'

'Yes', admitted Gerald sheepishly. 'I hoped so, but of course if it's out of the question, it doesn't matter. You're the best thing that's happened to me for ages. I still want you as a friend. I've acted like a spoilt child. Please, please forgive me.'

Wonderingly, Judith cradled his head on her shoulder. Then impulsively she lifted it and sought out his lips. 'Is this the sort of friendship you had in mind?' she murmured.

38

That night changed everything for Judith. It seemed the most natural thing in the world to make love to Gerald and when she awoke in the morning to find herself in his bed, it was as if a huge burden had been lifted from her shoulders. 'Happy?' he asked, smiling at her a little anxiously and holding her hand. 'Very', she replied firmly. 'I can't believe I've spent my life missing out on this.... I've never really done this before, you know.' Suddenly, she felt very shy. 'Was it all right? Was I… oh, you know what I mean, Gerald. I'm a professional virgin. And yet, it's so lovely being here with you… and doing this.' Gerald was kissing her neck. 'You were perfect', he said. 'I don't want you to do anything you don't want to. I will understand if this can't go on.'

'Would you like it to go on?'

'I can't think of anything I want more.'

'Perhaps I ought to tell you what that wretched newspaper story was all about in that case.'

'Only if you want to. Your past is your past as far as I'm concerned. This is your present – and mine. And, I hope, our future. All I can tell you is that I feel as if I've come home. I know that sounds corny but I've been so bitter and angry since Katie died. I didn't think I could love anyone again – and I know it's early days, but I already feel that it could be entirely possible with you. Perhaps you will with me, one day. Who knows? I was such a fool earlier; can you forgive me?'

'Of course,' said Judith reaching for him again. 'It must have been an unpleasant shock getting that anonymous letter. The ridiculous thing is that it isn't true.'

'How do you mean? You weren't in love with that woman?'

'No, not for a moment. It was the other way round. She fell in love with me – or so she said. She became obsessive. I was confused and I was flattered and since I'd never had a good experience with men, I thought there would be no harm in seeing whether it could work with her. She seduced me and one night, after a lot to drink, I let myself be seduced….'

'And…?'

'And, nothing. I was very fond of Veronica. It wasn't a bad experience, but it wasn't a good one either. And in the morning it became clear that it hadn't been a success and then it all turned sour. The next thing I knew, there was a scandal and Veronica betrayed me. She told the governors that I had tried to seduce her, that I was some kind of sexual predator, and produced some of my poems to back up her claim. They chose to believe her. Oh, Gerald, it was ghastly. So humiliating. I left the day I was accused and after that I fled here. I couldn't think of anything beyond getting as far away as possible. Thank god, I was in a position to be able to do it.'

'My poor darling', murmured Gerald. 'But that's terrible.'

'You do believe me, don't you?'

'Yes, of course I do. But what were these poems?'

'They were poems I had written and left lying about – she easily convinced everybody that they were intended for her – poems about love and loss and so on.'

'I didn't know you wrote poetry'.

'It's one of the many things you don't know about me,' whispered Judith, wrapping her legs around Gerald again.

Later, much later in the afternoon when they finally got dressed, and Gerald had begun to take in the exhilarating fact that his new love was also a published poet whom he had always admired, they discussed what they should do about Lance.

'I feel I'm polluting the atmosphere just talking about him,' said Judith. 'He's got away with everything so far – this letter he sent you is just typical of the man. He's pure evil, but it's probably best just to ignore it. After all, he hasn't done what he set out to achieve, has he? He hasn't turned you against me.'

Gerald was silent. He knew he couldn't leave it there. But he wasn't going to spoil things now. He would deal with Lance later. 'Let's have lunch and think about it,' he said.

'What about going down to the beach?'

'Perfect', replied Judith. 'And then back here for a siesta?'

As it happened, Tim beat Gerald to the recriminations. He felt wretched about unwittingly betraying Judith to Lance and was determined to make amends. That evening, after fortifying himself in the bar, he went over to Lance's house, ostensibly to pay him that month's rent.

When Lance finally opened the door to him, it was clear that he had been drinking heavily. 'Come in,' he slurred.

'I've come to give you my cheque for the rent,' said Tim, 'but I won't come in if you don't mind. The truth is, I've got a bone to pick with you Lance. That information I gave you about Judith Hay….'

'What of it? asked Lance aggressively.

'It wasn't for you to go and tell everybody about it. You must have known how damaging that would be for her.'

'Oh, I see,' said Lance, swaying rather alarmingly. 'It was fine for you to tell me, was it? But not for me to tell anyone else. In any case, I've only told one person – and that was in his best interests – that wanker Gerald whatisname from the bookshop.'

'Yes and Gerald phoned me up, understandably furious, telling me about the newspaper cutting and note you sent – he knew it was you – and so did I as soon as I heard about it. That was why you wanted to know which school Judith had taught at, wasn't it? So you could dredge up that story and send it to her friends? What's she ever done to you?' Tim thought, if he's going to be aggressive, so am I. He's stinking drunk and he's an even bigger asshole than I thought.

Lance lurched towards him, his face mottled and breath rancid. 'Look,' he shouted. 'I don't need some jumped up, wet-behind-the-ears little prick like you telling me what I can and can't do. Judith Hay has been making serious allegations about me and she deserves all she gets. And as for you…', he spluttered, 'you can go fuck yourself and you can get out of my *gîte* too while you're at it. You've got a week to clear out – and that's being generous. Now go!'

'I'm leaving anyway,' shouted Tim. 'I'm glad to get out of your *gîte*. I don't want to have any dealings with you in future.' Right, he thought, walking away quickly, that's it. I seem to be burning all my boats here. That morning he had spent with the police in Vevey giving them the details of his discovery of the wine stash and Roland's link to it. Roland had already been arrested apparently with his father, and he had seen that the wine cave had been cordoned off up in the hills. When he went to their café to see what was happening, it's shutters were down and it was closed up. In the village, knots of people were congregating, having heard the news no doubt. They stared at him in what he felt was a particularly hostile way. They were always staring, he thought, he was getting sick of it. He wondered what they felt about it all but somehow didn't the stomach to start interviewing any of them – in any case, his French wasn't good enough yet and he had a nasty feeling that they would almost certainly want to shoot the messenger.

He whistled for Piggy who was examining another dog's territorial marker. 'Come on girl, let's go to Auntie Fern's, shall we? How would you like to go and see England's green and pleasant land?' He wondered if Fern could possibly be persuaded to come back to England with him. They could set up some business together and Ben would certainly be happier. The poor boy had recovered some of his confidence but his friend Rose was about to go back to school in England and he was still finding French school difficult. He'd probably jump at the chance to go back to a sixth form college in England and get some A levels. He'd already complained to Tim that he didn't think he could hack the Bac, as he put it. And Fern – what of her? Their affair was still very new but Tim felt happier with her than he could recall ever feeling before. There was something deeply calming about Fern. Perhaps it was just that she was more grown up than him. She was vulnerable and yet strong; whereas he supposed he was almost exactly the opposite – strong (on the surface anyway) but vulnerable. Fern liked to look after him just as much he liked looking after her. They made a good team. She was a bit of an old hippy, but he liked that. She had definite views on everything and she seemed to have a real moral core which was unusual in Tim's circle of former friends. She was very sure of what was right and wrong in life and he admired that. None of his dippy, Sloaney girlfriends had ever given much thought to morality, or to anything other than sex and shopping come to that. He also was aware that Fern was anxious about his journalism and the trouble it landed him in. She feared that his thirst for a 'story' often overrode any principles. Like most people who weren't in the media, she distrusted it, and, who knows, thought Tim, maybe she was right. He had made a decent go of being a freelance out here but how many more stories were going to fall into his lap in this part of the world?

Gerald's method of dealing with Lance was more restrained but more deadly. He telephoned Lance that evening and told him that he would be filing a complaint against him for blackmail. Before Lance could slam the phone down on him, he also told him that rather more seriously, he knew that Lance was a sex pest – worse, a paedophile and possible rapist, and he would make sure everybody knew, he added.

Breathing heavily, Lance ended the call. He'd been a bloody fool. He could see that now. The sex thing could easily have been kept under wraps if he hadn't wilfully and maliciously wanted to make life difficult for the Hay woman. Nobody could possibly take Bill Bailey's accusations seriously, but if Thornton put it around that he was a some kind of pervert, people might start to talk. His reputation would be in ruins in no time and it was just possible, though unlikely, that the useless French police would take an interest. After all, there was no proof of anything and Sophie was safely out of the way in England. He had seen Camilla and Rex a couple of nights ago and they were as friendly as ever; she obviously hadn't mentioned anything to them.

But, he reasoned, probably the best thing for him now was to make a move. Jean had conveniently cleared off and he wasn't going to bother to find her. He'd been getting very bored with the parochial life down here for some time now. There was absolutely nobody around with whom he could have a civilised chat. And also, there was the small question of Roland, who, he had learnt that morning had been arrested and taken into custody. That had got him really worried. The rumour was going round that it was something to do with stolen wine; but if Roland was questioned about his other activities, then he, Lance, might very well be drawn into the investigation. Yes, it was definitely time to leave town – fortunately, he had a studio apartment in Paris that he could decamp to whilst he considered his future. He sighed heavily and poured himself another drink. Things did not look good, not good at all…

39

Later, Jean remembered nothing at all about her journey back from Oxford. Louise had been very kind beforehand – that she did recall. She made her stay for a while and kept fetching comforting cups of tea while Jean sobbed uncontrollably. 'I'm sorry, Louise,' she kept saying, 'it's you who should be crying; after all, you're the victim'.

'Jean, I did my crying a long time ago,' Louise had replied. 'In fact, if it makes you feel any better, in an odd way, I think that the shock I had then set me on course for becoming a doctor – which is the best thing I ever did. I was determined to take control of my life after that. I realised that if I could survive that, I could probably survive anything and that I could also do anything I put my mind to. I'd always set my heart on a medical career but I didn't have any confidence in myself. It sounds silly now, but once I got over it, I became a hell of a lot stronger on account of it. Of course, that doesn't go for everybody. Some people collapse after a shock; some ride the storm. I guess I was lucky.'

'You're a brave girl,' said Jean through her handkerchief. 'I can't bear to think of you having to keep that terrible secret to yourself – and of course Sarah too. Both of you trying to protect me, in a way. I suppose you never told your parents either?'

'No. I couldn't. There was too much shame and guilt and… I thought it would destroy them. I thought I could cope with it – and I did in the end. After all, I wasn't a very little girl; I was fifteen. I was innocent, but I was aware that Lance could argue that I'd led him on or some such thing. And Sarah half persuaded me that it was normal – that fathers, or some fathers, did that kind of thing all the time. I suppose she was right about that – not about it being normal, but about some fathers doing it all the time. Already I've had to deal with a few cases of child abuse in my surgery, and for those that I know about, there are probably dozens that I don't. She broke off and wiped her eyes.

'Don't,' cried Jean. 'I can't bear to hear about it. I feel soiled by association – ashamed. And especially ashamed of my own behaviour. I can see now that I should have spotted the warning signs… should have protected you and my own daughter… should have stood up to my husband. I won't ever be able to forgive myself.'

'I don't know about that,' smiled Louise. 'But, if I were you, I would do exactly what you're doing now. Search for Sarah, find Sarah and tell her you're sorry. She'll understand now that it's all behind her I'm sure. It's very important for both of you to find each other now. It's the only way forward.'

Beechcroft Road was not in the nice part of Wimbledon near the common. In fact, Tooting was perhaps a better description of where Sarah lived. Jean found the house easily enough the next day – a nondescript Victorian terrace house in a side street off a small parade of shabby shops. The house didn't look big enough to be divided into flats but there were two bells. Jean was trembling so much that she could hardly walk, let alone read the names on the bells. Fumbling in her bag for her spectacles, she felt a wave of nausea and panic sweep over her. Her legs began to buckle and she had to sit down suddenly on the low wall dividing 19 Beechcroft Road from its neighbour.

I don't know if I can go through with this, she thought. Her heart was thumping noisily and beads of sweat had broken out on her brow. Her hands were clammy. She realised she hadn't thought beyond this moment. What would she say to Sarah – if Sarah was still here. And would Sarah perhaps shut the door in her face? If that happened, then what? Would she recognise her daughter? Would Sarah recognise her… after all, she was a whole decade older – and probably looked more like two. That morning, she had dressed carefully wanting to look her best to meet her estranged daughter, recognising as she did so the absurdity of her actions. As if Sarah would care what she was wearing after all this time.

She found her spectacles and put them on her nose to peer at the bells. On the piece of paper Louise had given her it said Flat 2. But the bells weren't marked with numbers; there were just two names, neither of them Sarah's.

Just then, the front door opened and a young woman stood there with a small boy behind her. Wordlessly, they looked at each other. Minutes seemed to pass. Then Jean started to cry, silently, tears sliding down her cheeks and plopping into her open handbag. 'I knew you'd come,' said Sarah simply.

40

A little further away, in the next village, Tim was also woken up by the sirens and commotion. Flinging on some clothes, he looked out of the window and could see a dull red light over towards La Prairie. It looked as if there was a huge fire over there. His first thought was that it could be Roland's café. The police had told him that they had released Jean-Baptiste on bail on account of ill health and Tim had wondered what kind of reception he would receive locally. But surely, they wouldn't resort to burning his house down, would they?

He drove the four miles along the single track land to La Prairie like a madman, each mile bringing him closer to the heat and light. By the time he sped up the hill leading into the village, he could actually feel the heat and hear the ominous crackling of splintering timber. Scraps of blackened paper started to stick to the windscreen. It was impossible to get into the main square when he rounded the corner. Firemen had put up barricades but he could already see that the blaze was centred on Café Le Square.

Immediately, Tim knew that this fire was no accident. The release of Jean-Baptiste on bail and the rumour that

Jean-Baptiste had been a collaborator had whipped round the villages where everybody knew everybody else and many of the older ones recalled the train incident. Of course, the need for vengeance was strong and the French people, especially in rural areas, had no faith in their police system or in justice being done. It stood to reason that they had got revenge on the Chabots in their own way.

Tim felt sick. It was one thing bringing the Chabots to the attention of the law, quite another to get them incinerated. Horrified by the chain of events he had set in motion, he watched along with everyone else while the fireman hosed down the flames. It was clearly going to take all night and beyond. There was now almost a carnival atmosphere and people, some with small children, were chatting and laughing much as they did on market day. Knots of youths kept getting in the way of the firemen and one was kicked to the ground for his trouble. A fight broke out and everybody started shouting at once.

Appalled, Tim headed for home. There was nothing at all that he could do tonight. He would contact the police in the morning and try to find out exactly what happened. In the meantime, the best place for him was bed. Fern hadn't been around that evening and he had sat up late drinking on his own and pondering his future feeling depressed and trying to pack up his things. Lance had given him written notice to leave and he had to be out by the end of the week. Tonight's events had made matters even worse; he damn well wasn't going to file this as a newspaper story – it was too horrible, and he was to blame.

I'm going to quit journalism he thought, not for the first time. In fact I'm going to quit France. Something else that hasn't really worked out. He would take Piggy back to England with him – thank god that quarantine thing was over – and he was going to talk to Fern about everything in the morning. He wasn't sure how things stood with her. Their relationship was pretty new after all. She had settled down well in France now although he didn't think Ben was entirely happy. Would she want to come back with him and try to forge another new life?

The next morning, Tim was awoken by the telephone only a couple of hours after he had managed to fall asleep. Groping for the receiver as he lay on his stomach he finally located it, but not before knocking over a glass of water – 'Yes?' he shouted angrily into the phone. 'Morning Mr Lavery!' came the cheery response. 'I suppose you're on Midi time?' John Connelly, the Paris correspondent on the Sunday paper Tim worked for had taken to using Tim as his stringer in the south of France when he couldn't be bothered to chase up stories himself. 'Fuck off, John' muttered Tim. 'I've only had two hours' sleep. What the hell is it?'

'Nice way to talk to your senior colleagues,' said Connelly smoothly. 'Haul your ass out of bed. The editor wants you to follow up some story about a Nazi wine loot and wartime collaborators down in your neck of the woods.' Tim sat up in bed. 'How did you know about that?' he asked. 'Picked it up from the local rag down there – surprised you didn't tell us about it.', Connelly replied.

'That's because it's my fucking story', said Tim 'which I wanted to do more work on first. As a matter of fact, the story has grown bigger overnight. The collaborator was murdered by the locals who burned his house down last night. That good enough for you?'

'Well I'd get on with it, mate, if I were you,' said Connelly. 'It all sounds good boondock stuff to me – they never really got over the war down there, did they? Only you'd better file it before the dailies start sniffing around. Thank God, it's Saturday. They can run it tomorrow. Makes a change from overbrimming morgues up here.'

Hell, thought Tim, furiously. Now I've got to run the story. I may want to quit journalism, but it doesn't want to quit me. He stumbled out of bed and into the shower. By the time he came out dripping and downed a reviving glass of orange juice, he felt rather better. Suppressing his conscience about Jean-Baptiste, he tried to concentrate on the positive aspects of the story – which, after all, was a bloody good one – and one that he had orchestrated himself. He reckoned with the latest developments it would make a centre-page spread. The English papers loved sensational French murder stories and anything to do with Nazis had the editor salivating. Humming tunelessly, he hurriedly dressed and prepared to go back to the fire scene and then start interviewing the police. He'd have to tell Fern he couldn't make that picnic on the beach this afternoon.

Tim's story in the Sunday paper made it on to front page as well as the main spread in the weekend review section. France was very much in the news because of the disastrous effects of the heat wave there and, as Tim had predicted, there was nothing the editor liked better than a scandal involving the French, the war and collaborators. They went strong on the angle that it was their own reporter, Tim Lavery, who had first discovered and then alerted the authorities to the wine hoard and it was padded out with all sorts of boxed information about the war, the region and the wine which had now been shipped to experts for a valuation and was expected to make vast amounts of money when auctioned off – after all the legal wrangles concerning ownership.

There was a macabre grainy photograph of firemen removing what were assumed to be the remains of Jean-Baptiste Chabot from his house above the restaurant and a think piece by the Paris correspondent about the recent wave of anti-British sentiment in the area. On the Saturday night before it ran, the editor himself telephoned Tim in France to congratulate him. 'Brilliant stuff,' he said. 'We want more of that kind of thing. Can you dig up a few more collaborators do you think?'

'Actually, I'm thinking of coming back to England,'

confessed Tim. 'I'm fed up with France and I'm thinking about a fresh start. I've been thrown out of my accommodation and, as you can imagine, I'm not exactly Mr Popular around here.'

'Any plans back here?' asked the editor.

'I don't know,' said Tim. 'I was thinking that maybe I should try something other than journalism.'

'Don't be ridiculous', was the reply. 'You're on the up, old chap. If you come back now I can guarantee a role for you on our new Probe section – remember the old Insight team on the Sunday Times? Well, we're setting up a crack investigative team here just like that to dig up just the kind of thing you've done in France – Scams, sex scandals, old feuds, child molesters in high places... what about it? You've got my word, you'll be on the team. Job security, good salary, interesting work... what do you say?'

'Yes', said Tim helplessly. 'Thanks, that sounds great'.

'Good. When can you start?'

'Next week?'

Relief flooded through him. And the decision had been practically taken for him – no arsing about now, wondering what the hell to do. Hey, things were looking good and it would be wonderful to back in London again... now that he thought about it, he missed it terribly. And his mum would be pleased. It was a minute or so before he thought of Fern. Shit! What would she say? It was bad timing to have just started an affair with her – and Ben would be very pissed off with him leaving town just like that too. If only he could persuade them to come with him – they could all have a fresh start.

41

On the 18th of August, the Surgeon-General Lucien Abenheim resigned having appeared to be completely unprepared for the unseasonably high temperatures and the chaos that ensued. France requested aid from the European Union and the government came under heavy criticism for its handling of the crisis. According to some reports, the absence of doctors on August leave were amongst the contributing factors to the high number of deaths as well as a failure of communication and imagination within the health and social networks. By the end of August, the heat wave had killed a total of 14,800 people – a death rate sixty percent higher than average for that time of year.

The worst of it was the number of bodies left unclaimed, presumably because their relations were still away on the immutable French August holiday. In Paris, where the problem was the most acute, there were medieval scenes as those shifting makeshift coffins into temporary morgues were having to wear masks to protect them from the stench of rotting corpses.

*

When the body of a middle-aged rather overweight man was found in a side street in late August off the rue de l'université, it was bundled unceremoniously into the back of an undertaker's van along with others and taken to a nearby temporary morgue –another victim of the heat wave. A cursory search had produced no identification beyond a credit card from a French bank but sporting an English-sounding name. It was to be over a week before the overburdened authorities notified the bank and a further two weeks before admittedly leisurely detective work established that the wife of the deceased was now in London and she was contacted. Even the hardened police sergeant of the 7th *arrondissement* whose task it was to tell Jean Campion that the heat wave appeared to have claimed her husband, was slightly shocked to hear the note of relief in her voice. And so it was that Lance Campion became another statistic – an apparently neglected person whose family hadn't cared enough to check up on them.

In fact Lance's demise was nothing to do with the heat wave and everything to do with one of Paris's other less attractive problems – the fifteen tonnes of dog shit dumped on its streets by its population of 200,000 dogs which regularly lands over 650 Parisians a year in hospital. Lance's misfortune had been to skid in a freshly laid heap of dung and crack his head open on a fire hydrant – an undignified way to go, as he would have been the first to note.

*

On the day that Lance came to an untimely end, Judith was helping Gerald pack up at Wuthering Heights. In a remarkably short space of time, he had managed to sell the lease on the shop and sell the book stock on to another English bookshop in Nimes. He and Judith would be leaving France at the end of August and had rented a flat in central London where they would live until they found somewhere to buy together, once Judith's house in La Prairie was sold.

As she stacked books in crates, Judith thought, as she did all the time now, about her change in fortune and circumstance. What a difference a month makes! From frowsy spinster to frothy fiancée! She couldn't quite believe how effortlessly she had adjusted to the clutter and clamour of living with someone else after the single, abstemious life. It hadn't felt like it at the time, but Judith saw, now that she had something with which to compare it, what an unanchored life she had been leading with no parents, no children and no partner to shape and define her. She marvelled at her new-found sense of security with Gerald; suddenly, it was unthinkable to have been alone for so long.

And Gerald, too, had visibly mellowed and relaxed. Customers in his shop who had been a little wary of him and thought him a bit of a curmudgeon, noticed how genial and relaxed he was these days. Living with Judith suited him very well indeed. After his wife had died far too early of cancer, he had been certain that he would be alone for the rest of his life and had convinced himself that because this was inevitable, that it was for the best. His depth of feeling for Judith and the speed at which their relationship had progressed astonished him. It all just felt so right.

Both of them were old enough to know that the first heady months of sexual attraction would wear off at some point but that the comfort of companionship and compatibility would sustain them in the future. Both were looking forward to a new life together in England. Judith wanted to go back to teaching and Gerald thought he could set up again as an independent publisher. They had been over to London for a week to find somewhere to live and whilst they were there had arranged to be married at Marylebone Register Office at the end of September. They didn't want any fuss. Only Judith's old friend Jane and Gerald's brother, Francis, would be witnesses. They would put a notice in The Times announcing that the marriage had taken place and that would be it.

Their final act, once Wuthering Heights was emptied and locked up, was to take down the Union Jack which had signalled to the world that there had been an English corner of Montpellier. When Gerald had set up shop ten years previously, it was the only British flag to be seen in town; now union jacks were a common enough sight fluttering outside English tea rooms, English pubs and even one English restaurant presided over by two stout red-cheeked ladies from Worcestershire who bravely attempted to titillate the French palette with Steak and Kidney pie and apple crumble. Against all the odds, it was doing rather well.

*

'We won't need this where we're going,' remarked Gerald, taking down the flag and preparing to put it in with the rubbish. 'Keep it for luck', replied Judith, putting out a restraining arm. 'After all, it led me to you.'

Afterwards

London, October

Veronica Templeton and her new close companion Margaret Cook were having a coffee in Sloane Square on a rare weekend off prior to doing some shopping in Peter Jones. Margaret Cook was a maths teacher at The Chase who had been appointed a couple of months after Judith Hay had unceremoniously left the school. A big-boned woman in her early forties, she, like Judith before her, had been captivated by her new headmistress and this time Veronica's physical overtures were not rebuffed. After Judith went, Veronica was badly in need of succour though this time she was determined to be more discreet. Margaret Cook didn't make her heart beat faster as Judith had done, but she was a dependable friend and a surprisingly adept lover. 'Look at this,' Margaret said now, pointing to a notice in The Times which she was reading while scoffing a croissant. There were crumbs and grease stains all over the Court Circular page. 'Isn't that the woman who left the school so suddenly?'

Veronica had been deliberately vague about Judith Hay

and her reasons for leaving. She looked now where Margaret's stubby, tobacco-stained index finger pointed and found herself reading the marriage notice informing her that the wedding had quietly taken place of Mr Gerald Thornton, formerly of Montpellier, France, and Miss Judith Hay, formerly of Warwickshire. Veronica felt as though someone had delivered a blow to her stomach and her eyes involuntarily filled up. 'Yes, I think so,' she managed in a strangled voice. 'I didn't think she was the marrying kind,' said Margaret with a laugh, but Veronica had already hurriedly left her seat and was heading for the Ladies, her face wet with unexpected tears.

Tim Lavery was enjoying his new job as part of the Probe team, and particularly enjoying his enhanced earnings. However, it was bloody hard work and already he missed the more relaxing lifestyle that he had left behind in the south of France. More particularly, he missed Fern and Ben. Fern had refused to uproot herself again just as she had settled down and didn't want to pull Ben out of French school in his Baccalaureate year. It was entirely understandable, thought Tim, but he was pretty low about them not being there just the same. He greatly missed Piggy too. In the rush that followed his leaving France, Fern had agreed to look after her until Tim could make arrangements for her to come to London.

Idly, he flicked through the London evening paper to see

if there was anything worth seeing at the cinema. As he did so, a by line in the paper on a down-page story about a missing woman about caught his eye. 'By Carinthia Greene' it read. My God, thought Tim, recalling the insouciant long-legged schoolgirl whose willing co-operation with him on that long ago story about The Chase led to his downfall, – there can't be two of them. He might have known it though. Carinthia had been a natural for a journalist, and he wouldn't have put it past her to have blagged her way into a reporter's job with the *Evening News*. Grinning to himself, he reached for the phone.

Mrs Thornton, as Judith now took some pride in thinking of herself, sat in a small Italian restaurant off Kensington High Street looking rather nervously about her. She was waiting for Jean Campion. Like everyone else who knew him, she had been at first astonished when she read Lance's obituary in the newspaper, and then rather ashamed of herself at how little compassion she could summon up for his passing. It seemed incredible that her old adversary was dead, struck down by nothing more malicious than a heat wave. Her first thought had been of Jean, whom she had not seen since the fateful evening after the meeting in Vevey, when Jean had publicly broken free of her husband and confessed her fears for her daughter Sarah. Jean had been a broken woman then, but Judith suspected, rightly, that she was about to turn her life around.

With difficulty, but with the help of some mutual friends in France, she had tracked Jean down to her current number in London and rang to express her shock and sympathy, if that was the right word. 'I'm back in London now,' she explained to Jean who had been touched to hear from her and delighted by her own good news. Lance, she said, had been brought back to be buried in Hertfordshire where he had grown up. It had been a simple ceremony with a few of his old friends in attendance. She had gone to pay her last respects, but it had been very painful, and she had felt a hypocrite. The better news, she told Judith on the phone, was that she had been reunited with Sarah which had been both difficult and joyous in equal measure. 'Now, it's as if we've never been apart,' she said, her voice catching with emotion. 'Sarah is really grounded and working in an art gallery and I see a great deal of her. I'm so much happier to be back here now.' And what of you? Judith had asked. 'Oh I've got plenty to keep me busy,' replied Jean enigmatically. 'Let's meet, and I'll tell you all about it.'

And so here Judith was looking up at everyone who came into the restaurant and hoping that the Jean she was about to see was really a happier woman than the one she had known in France. The door opened and Jean walked in, smiling in happy anticipation. The two women embraced and then Jean began to explain about the small boy she had in tow. 'I hope you don't mind,' she said, 'I've brought Joe, my grandson, with me as he's got an unexpected half day at school – something to do with a teachers' strike – he's very good in restaurants and he'll be happy to sit here with us and have a pizza.'

'Of course I don't mind,' said Judith. 'But I didn't realise you had a grandson… oh…,' the truth dawning, 'is he Sarah's son?' She turned to greet Joe properly. 'Hi Joe…', she started, then stopped suddenly, blood rushing to her face when she saw his distinctive, unmistakable pale eyes. 'Yes,' said Jean calmly, watching her. 'I knew you would know when you saw him. It is what you think. It's taken me a long time, but I'm over the shock now. He's such a dear little boy…', she put her hand to her throat and her eyes watered a little. 'Run over there,' she said to Joe now 'and see if you can find us some menus.' She watched as Joe skipped over towards the counter. 'He's himself,' she said, composing herself and turning back to Judith, 'he's Joe, he's gorgeous and I love him dearly.